PENGUIN CLASSICS

REVERIES OF THE SOLITARY WALKER

JEAN-JACQUES ROUSSEAU was born in Geneva in 1712, the son of an artisan. His mother died a few days after his birth, his father was exiled when he was ten. After a period as apprentice to an engraver, he left the city in 1728; thereafter he led a wandering life in France, Switzerland, Savoy and Italy, trying many trades, and living for many years as the protégé (and briefly the lover) of Madame de Warens at Chambéry. In 1742 he went to Paris, hoping to make his way in the world; in the next few years he was secretary to the French Ambassador in Venice and to a rich Parisian family. He also made friends with the philosopher Diderot, for whose *Encyclopedia* he wrote several articles, particularly on musical subjects (he was subsequently to have great success as a composer). In 1744 he began his liaison with Thérèse Levasseur, which lasted until his death. His denunciation of the corruption of modern civilization, the *Discourse on the Sciences and the Arts* (1751), brought him instant fame, and the following years saw a succession of major works which develop a powerful critique of contemporary society and put forward ideas for the moral and social regeneration of humanity: the *Letter to d'Alembert on the Theatre*, the *Discourse on Inequality*, *Émile* (on education), the *Social Contract* and the immensely popular novel, *La Nouvelle Héloïse*. The logic of his ideas led Rousseau to withdraw from Parisian society, living in the country, attempting to earn his living as a music copyist and breaking with such friends and allies as Voltaire and Diderot. The scandal caused by his defence of natural religion in *Émile* forced him to flee from France in 1762; for the next few years he was hounded from place to place, living successfully in Switzerland, England and the French provinces. He returned to Paris in 1770 and remained there until shortly before his death in 1778. In his final years he produced a remarkable series of autobiographical writings, all of them published posthumously, the *Confessions*, the *Dialogues* and the *Reveries of the Solitary Walker*.

PETER FRANCE is Professor of French at the University of Edinburgh. He studied modern languages at Magdalen College, Oxford, and from 1963 until 1980 taught in the School of European Studies at the University of Sussex. His publications include books on French literature of the *ancien régime*, editions of English and French texts, and translations of Diderot's *Letters to Sophie Volland* and of modern Russian poetry.

Jean-Jacques Rousseau

REVERIES OF
THE SOLITARY WALKER

TRANSLATED
WITH AN INTRODUCTION BY
PETER FRANCE

PENGUIN BOOKS

Penguin Books Ltd, Harmondsworth, Middlesex, England
Viking Penguin Inc., 40 West 23rd Street, New York, New York 10010, U.S.A.
Penguin Books Australia Ltd, Ringwood, Victoria, Australia
Penguin Books Canada Limited, 2801 John Street, Markham, Ontario, Canada L3R 1B4
Penguin Books (N.Z.) Ltd, 182–190 Wairau Road, Auckland 10, New Zealand

—

This translation first published 1979
Reprinted 1981, 1984, 1986, 1987

—

Copyright © Peter France, 1979
All rights reserved

—

Printed and bound in Great Britain by
Cox & Wyman Ltd, Reading
Set in Monotype Bembo

CONTENTS

INTRODUCTION

JEAN-JACQUES ROUSSEAU has suffered more than most writers from the dismemberment inflicted by the categories of library catalogues. All too often different specialists will read *Émile* (on education), *The Social Contract* (on politics) or even *Julie* (a novel) in isolation from one another. *Reveries of the Solitary Walker* is not a book for specialists. It does not deal explicitly with all the various questions raised in the earlier works, but it takes the reader straight to the heart of its author's main concerns and beliefs. And perhaps even more important, it gives us the characteristic manner and tone which, directly or indirectly, reveal the man himself and all his contradictions.

It was in the autumn of 1776 that Rousseau began what was to be his last book. He was sixty-four, and had just emerged from one of the darkest passages of his life. In 1762, after a period of just over ten years in which he had produced a resounding series of doctrinal, prophetic and imaginative writings, he had been virtually exiled from France, principally on account of the unorthodox religion professed in *Émile*. Thereafter his existence had been one of wandering and self-justification, haunted by a growing sense that he was the victim of a universal conspiracy. Much of this was the work of his frenzied imagination; at the time when he saw himself as cast out by human society, he was in fact loved, admired and revered by many of his contemporaries. Nevertheless, there were also very real causes for suffering – the hostility and contempt of former friends, the outlawing of books that he saw as a passionate contribution to the public good, and, perhaps bitterest of all, the rejection and condemnation of himself and his writings in his idealized fatherland, Geneva.

After taking refuge successively in the Neuchâtel region of Switzerland, England, and various parts of France, Rousseau had finally come back to Paris in 1770. By now he was the object of immense curiosity, and indeed one of the most famous names in Europe, so much so that he was known simply as Jean-Jacques; he was one of the earliest examples of Carlyle's new category, the Hero as Man of Letters. Even so, he lived quietly with his companion Thérèse in a modest apartment in the Rue Plâtrière near the Palais-Royal, copying music for a living and occupying his free time with writing, music, botany and country walks until a few weeks before his death. In May 1778 he accepted the Marquis de Girardin's invitation to settle on his estate at Ermenonville, and it was here that he died in July of that year.

The months before he began the *Reveries* seem to have been especially black. Over the previous four years he had written a fascinating and extravagant sequel to his earlier *Confessions*, the *Dialogues* (also known as *Rousseau, the Judge of Jean-Jacques*). Here he had tried to demonstrate his integrity against the charge that he was a false prophet whose hypocritical preaching was belied by his degraded life. Believing himself encircled in an impenetrable conspiracy of silence and misrepresentation, he had attempted in vain to deposit the manuscript of the *Dialogues* on the high altar of Notre Dame, had then given copies of it to the philosopher Condillac and an English visitor, and finally, despairing of ever making his voice heard, had tried to hand out to passers-by a hand-written circular beginning:

To all Frenchmen who still love justice and truth.
People of France! Nation that was once kind and affectionate, what has become of you? Why have you changed towards an unfortunate foreigner who is alone, at your mercy, without any support or defender ...

It is hard to avoid adjectives like 'pathetic' or 'mad' in describing such behaviour. But of course this was not Rousseau's constant condition. In particular, it seems (and he himself claimed) that some time in the summer of 1776 he regained a degree of serenity; the First Walk in the *Reveries* speaks of a mysterious 'event as sad as it was unexpected' which had left him in a state of 'total calm'. At all events, when he was visited in early August by the Englishman Thomas Bentley, he seems to have been in full possession of his faculties. In his diary Bentley recounts a conversation which ranges over the American Declaration of Independence, questions of religion and morality, fossils and the origin of the globe, and the birds which fly in at the window to be fed, and concludes with this description of Rousseau:

He is a musical instrument above the concert pitch, and therefore too elevated for the present state of society, and all his singularities and errors, as they are called, proceed from the extreme delicacy of his sensations.

I was so taken up with his intellect that I have almost forgot how it was clothed, though I remember he has a small slender body, rather below the common size, that he has a thin palish face with delicate features, and that he has a great deal of expression in his eyes and countenance when he is either pleased or displeased, one of which he certainly is every moment, for nothing that he sees or hears or thinks of is indifferent to him. When Nature was making this singular being, one would imagine she intended him for an inhabitant of the air, but before she had finished his wings he eagerly sprung out of her hands, and his unfinished body sunk him down to the earth.

Bentley's account tallies well with the better-known descriptions given by other companions of Rousseau's declining years, particularly that of Bernardin de Saint-Pierre. Bernardin also paints a rather idyllic picture of his hero's simple surroundings in 1772:

Near him stood a little spinet on which he tried out a tune now and then. Two little beds with covers of blue and white striped cotton like the wall-hangings, a chest of drawers, a table and a few chairs were all his furniture. On the walls were a plan of the forest and park of Montmorency, where he had lived, and an engraving of the King of England, his former benefactor. His wife sat sewing linen, a canary sang in a cage hanging from the ceiling, sparrows came and ate bread-crumbs at his windows which opened on to the street, and on the window-sill of the antechamber stood boxes and pots full of the sort of plants that Nature is pleased to sow.

Rousseau had moved to another apartment in the same street in between times, but it was probably in a room like this that in 1776 he began the *Reveries*. The chronology of the work is uncertain, but it seems that the first two Walks were written in the autumn and winter of that year and the next five before the end of the following summer; then there was a break and a new beginning in the winter of 1777–8, the Eighth Walk returning to some of the themes of the First. The Ninth came fairly soon after, and the Tenth is dated Palm Sunday 1778. For the first seven there is a fair copy in Rousseau's hand, but the Eighth and Ninth have been edited from rough drafts and the Tenth is unfinished. The book was first published in 1782, four years after the author's death.

*

The *Reveries* is the work of a man who lost no opportunity of declaring his dislike of books and book-writers. His visitors at the Rue Plâtrière were often told that he no longer read books, and in the Second Walk we see him rebuffing a well-wisher with the information that he 'receives no authors'. This was no new development in his life. The work which brought him fame in 1751, the *Discourse on the Sciences and the Arts*, is a paradoxically literary declamation against the cor-rupting influence of the arts, learning and literature. Later writings tell a similar story: in *Émile* he suggests that the profession of author is an unnecessary and even harmful luxury trade, like that of goldsmith, and in the *Dialogues* he protests that although he has written books he is not a book-writer. He often describes his entry into the world of literature as a terrible mistake. In order to protect his amateur status he insists that his real profession is music-copying, for it is above all the professional writers who are corrupt. These are the vain people who, as he says in the Third Walk, 'merely wanted to write a book, any book, so long as it was successful'. His own books he presents as the opposite of such futile performances: his early work was the inspired prophecy of a man with a burning message for the world, and his later autobiographical writing the necessary self-defence of a persecuted man.

In spite of these protestations, Rousseau clearly loved books; if they are the mark of civilized corruption, then he too was corrupted. Even in the *Discourse on the Sciences and the Arts* he excepts a few great men from his sweeping condemnation of contemporary culture; similarly, in *Émile*, he sings the praises of the children's bible, *Robinson Crusoe*, and in the fourth of his Walks he declares his abiding love of Plutarch. But quite apart from these favourites he was a very widely read man, and one who had thought a great deal about writing. His contemporaries admired his prose style in a way that embarrassed him, since it could be thought to detract from the seriousness of his message. Even so, he did not mind taking on the role of literary expert now and again, and he obviously took great pleasure in the well-shaped sentence, and indeed in the act of writing itself. His novel *Julie* seems to have given him great imaginative pleasure; when it was written he treated it as a favourite child, having it printed and bound as beautifully as possible. The preface to the novel admits the paradox of the writer who scorns books, and begins with the words: 'Big cities need plays and corrupt people need novels. I have seen the manners of my time and I have published these letters. Would that I had lived in an age when I should have had to burn them!' The man who often spoke like Savonarola knew quite well that he was living in a world of books – there was no going back to lost innocence.

And so it is that as an old man he is not content to walk in the country, study flowers, make music and talk, but once again begins to write. So it is that he says of his stay on the Island of Saint-Pierre, the scene of some of his least bookish experiences, 'I could have written one [a book] about every grass in the meadows, every moss in the woods, every lichen covering the rocks.' What could this vice of writing do for him then? What need had he to *write* the *Reveries*?

The answer can only be guessed at, and is probably not a simple one. In the First Walk, Rousseau cites one of the nearest parallels to his enterprise, the *Essays* of Montaigne, echoes of which are to be found throughout the book. Both are attempts to portray the changing mind of their authors. 'I describe not the essence but the passage,' wrote Montaigne (in Florio's English), and Rousseau's title suggests something of the same variable and vagabond quality. In my translation I have deliberately left the word 'reverie' as it is in the French, since so much of the work is devoted to exploring this state of mental wandering – in a telling phrase jotted down on a playing-card at the time when he was writing this book, Rousseau says: 'My whole life has been little else than a long reverie divided into chapters by my daily walks.' Or again, he says in the First Walk that his aim is 'to give an account of the successive variations of my soul', something like a series of barometer readings.

Although Rousseau claims to be keeping this record not for others but for himself, unlike Montaigne, it is hard to take this at face value when so much of the book seems to be devoted to a final attempt to set the record straight. The disregard for the opinion of others is never as complete as he would have wished. But those who keep diaries will know that there is a sense in which Rousseau's statement is true: he is writing to prolong the memory of reveries past and present and of the circumstances that produced them. As he writes he renews the pleasure of reverie and builds up a store of pleasure for himself in his declining years – it is part of the art of enjoying life which mattered so much to him.

Day-dreaming is one thing, writing is another. Indeed, the reader will quickly realize that this book is far from being simply 'a faithful record of my solitary walks and the reveries that occupy them'. How could it be? Not many of the Walks are directly concerned with walks around Paris, though they may record some of the thoughts that filled Rousseau's head as he walked (see, for instance, the beginning of the Fourth Walk). Most of them are discussions of one particular topic, and although the movement from one to the next may be capricious, the actual organization of each piece is quite unlike the wandering associative pattern of reverie as it is described in the Fifth Walk. The Fourth is probably the most highly structured of all; it poses a question and then deals with its various ramifications in a methodical way, answering possible objections, giving examples and eventually reaching the sought-after conclusion. Much more obviously than Montaigne, Rousseau seems to be intent here on sorting things out and reaching a stable position which he can defend against the attacks of his 'enemies'. In the other Walks the reasoning process is perhaps less obtrusive, but all of them are clearly and persuasively structured and show their author consciously reflecting on some of the major preoccupations of his life and earlier writing.

If the ordering of material is not as vague and drifting as the title may suggest, neither is the style. Rousseau and his readers set great store by the cadences of his prose, but this harmony does not seem to have come easily to him; in the first book of the *Confessions* he writes: 'There are some of my sentences that I have turned over and over in my head for five or six nights on end before they were fit to be committed to paper.' My experience as a translator seems to confirm that the language of the *Reveries*, far from being the natural jottings of a dreamer, is the result of careful and elaborate construction. Take the famous paragraph in the Fifth Walk beginning: 'But if there is a state where the soul can find a resting-place ...' Here all the resources of traditional prose eloquence – and one or two besides – are deployed to create elaborate and compelling sentences which will evoke a piece of the past with great power and fix it for ever. It is the answer to the anxiety betrayed in the preceding paragraph: 'Everything is in constant flux on this earth.' In the many repetitions, the symmetrical groupings and the cadences of his long sentences, it is as if Rousseau were building himself a refuge from the attacks of others and from his own fears and doubts.

Again and again in the *Reveries* we come across this idea of the refuge, the stable resting-place; the old and anxious author seems to be reassuring himself (or us) that he has at last recovered or discovered the secure peace he longs for. And yet this very repetition and the eloquence with which he creates and conveys this sense of security alert us to the fragility of his construction. To be sure, there are passages of ecstasy and tranquillity in the ten Walks, and taken as a whole the book is more serene than the preceding *Dialogues*. At the same time it is a worried book; full of obsession with enemies and extravagant protestations of innocence, it breathes self-doubt, self-pity and self-aggrandizement. Clearly it was not in Jean-Jacques' power totally to quell the contradictory fears and desires that had shaped his life – indeed a great part of his achievement is to have expressed so powerfully the difficulty of living in society and the conflicting aspirations that have come to occupy so large a place in modern life and literature. To help the reader to understand these emotions and ideas more clearly, I should like now to look briefly at his earlier writings and the image of his life given by his *Confessions*. In doing so, I shall focus on the tug-of-war between solitude and society, which I see as his central theme.

*

Rousseau was not a Frenchman, he was a Genevan. In reply to Geneva's condemnation of his books he renounced his citizenship in 1763, but until then he was proud to call himself 'Rousseau, Citizen of Geneva'. In France he often felt like an outsider; not only was he a foreigner, but unlike most other writers he was the son of an artisan and had not been given a regular education. It is not surprising that he often idealized the birthplace he had left as a latter-day Sparta, a simple, unspoilt place where the old community spirit had not yet succumbed to the Athenian corruption of Paris. Several times he imagines how his life might have gone had he remained among his own people, an obscure citizen plying the trade of his fathers; thus in the *Confessions*, 'I should have been a good Christian, a good father, a good friend, a good worker, a good man in every way.'

But of course he did leave his city, and lived for most of his adult life in France, an absent citizen. And even before this his sense of belonging to a secure community must have been disturbed in several ways. His mother died when he was a few days old. His father, with whom he had read the old French romances and Plutarch, went into self-imposed exile as the result of a quarrel when Jean-Jacques was ten. So the boy was left virtually an orphan, and after a happy spell under the care of a Protestant minister he was apprenticed to an engraver who apparently dealt with him roughly and tyrannically. Eventually, by an accident which is described in the *Confessions* as if it were the stroke of Destiny, he found himself at the age of fifteen locked out of Geneva after sundown one night, and rather than go back to his master he chose like his father to go into exile.

It would take too long to follow him on the paths of exile, which are wonderfully evoked in the *Confessions*. We read in these pages of his joy in being free and alone, already the solitary walker and a sort of super-tramp as he walks across the Alps to Turin and back and subsequently to Paris and back. One passage in the *Confessions* (written long after the event, in the 1760s) describes a night by the river near Lyon which prefigures the lonely ecstasies of the *Reveries* – even if the last sentence suggests that solitude is a second-best at this time:

It had been very hot that day, the evening was delightful; the parched grass was damp with dew; it was a quiet windless night; the air was cool yet not cold; the sunset had left red vapours in the sky, whose reflections tinged the water pink; the trees on the terraces were full of nightingales answering one another. I walked around in a kind of ecstasy, abandoning all my senses and my heart to the enjoyment of it all, yet sighing a little that I was alone in enjoying it.

For all this, Rousseau was a young man who had to make a living for himself, finding work or patrons and learning to get on with other people. Again, the *Confessions* gives a striking account of his varied relations with his peers, with protectors, with women. It is hard to tell from pages written so long after the event how quickly he developed the extreme susceptibility to the opinions and attitudes of others which made his later life so miserable. He must always have been a volatile and excitable person, quick to sense hostility or contempt, unwilling to be dominated, and never very easy to live with. His writings suggest the recurrent need to recreate the relations of perfect trust and transparency which the orphan and exile necessarily lacked. Whether they derived from Plutarch and the old romances, of from a sense of personal deprivation, his demands on human society were unusually great, so that when they were frustrated he was often driven to find satisfaction in the life of the imagination.

To judge from the *Confessions* and the Tenth Walk of the *Reveries*, it would seem that for a short time he was able to be fully himself while living in harmony with someone else. This was the period he spent with Madame de Warens, his first protector, with whom he lived as man and wife at Chambéry or, in the near-by countryside, at 'Les Charmettes'. She was twelve years his senior; he called her 'Mamma' and she called him 'Little One'. If we are to believe his retrospective accounts, his life with her was one of harmony with the world and with another person such as he subsequently had to create for himself in his imagination and in books.

The idyll came to an end. By the time he became known as a writer in 1751 Rousseau had been living for some years in the city which he often presents as the anti-Geneva, Paris. Here he knew many people and was involved, for instance, in the great common enterprise of the *Encyclopedia*, edited principally by his friend Denis Diderot. This does not seem to have given him a sense of real community. Neither does his long-lasting relationship with Thérèse Levasseur: she looked after him and was often a comfort to him, and during his exile he eventually declared that she was his wife, but it does not seem that she ever came near to being what Madame de Warens had been for him. According to Rousseau, his children by Thérèse were placed in the Paris Foundlings' Home.

So it is that in the *Confessions* Rousseau gives the impression that he was lost in this society, held by it but not at home in it, wandering in Dante's dark wood as he reached the middle of his life. Then, in the 1750s, he tried to break out of this alien world, and to formulate in writing his criticism of it and the possible escape-routes, whether into solitude or into a re-generated society. What he was trying to escape from is perhaps most memorably stated in the early pages of *Émile*, the book on education which he said was the keystone of his philosophical edifice:

Dragged along contrary roads by nature and by men, forced to divide ourselves between these different impulses, we follow a path of compromise which leads us to neither of our goals. So we are tossed about as long as we live, and we die without having been able to reconcile ourselves with ourselves and without serving either ourselves or other people.

An earlier work, the *Discourse on Inequality*, had put forward a hypothesis to account for humanity's present discontents. Unlike almost all his contemporaries, Rousseau declares that our natural state is solitude. His natural man and woman walk alone through the fertile forests, not speaking and meeting only for as long as is necessary for procreation; they are guided in their actions by the instinct of self-preservation, which is mitigated as in some other animals by a natural unwillingness to inflict suffering. To use a distinction which is important for Rousseau's self-description in the *Reveries*, natural man and woman are *good*, since they have no desire to harm others, but they cannot yet be *virtuous*, since virtue implies a conscious altruism that is only possible once society, language, rational thought and morality have developed. Similarly natural human beings, created largely out of Jean-Jacques' introspection, are free of the desire to change their condition. Like the other animals they exert themselves to satisfy their real needs; otherwise, they are happy to live in idleness.

In this view, which is more mythical than historical, it was only by some obscure accident that we ever came to live in society and develop the social potential that was in our solitary forebears. So Rousseau is able to attribute to society not only such human achievements as the development of morality, the invention of speech, writing, agriculture and all the arts and sciences, but also all the evils of inequality and domination which accompany them. In particular he sees the natural instinct for self-preservation or love of self (*amour de soi*) being transformed into the competitive, self-regarding spirit which he calls *amour-propre* and which I have translated here as 'self-love'. Among other things this theory provided an explanation for the vanity and extreme self-consciousness which he felt in himself, allowing him to believe that these were not his real self, but a social deformation of it.

At different times Rousseau gave different weight to the good and evil of the social state (Chapter 8 of the first book of the *Social Contract* celebrates the advantages of society). But in any case, given that this secular version of the Fall had occurred and society had developed with all its achievements and miseries, how were Jean-Jacques and his contemporaries to find their way to a state which offered some of the advantages of our supposed natural state? *Émile* suggests that there is a radical choice to be made between living entirely for oneself and devoting oneself to the community: 'Obliged to combat either nature or social institutions, we must choose between creating a man or a citizen, for one cannot create both at the same time.'

In a late work, his *Considerations on the Government of Poland*, Rousseau imagines a Polish society of patriots, not unlike ancient Sparta, where everything private is subordinated to the common interest. More generally however, starting from the corrupt and divided societies he knew, where he saw no possibility of reviving true patriotism, he opted for some sort of compromise between the non-existent state of natural solitude and the ideal community he sometimes dreamed of. Already in the *Discourse on Inequality* he had written of a historical 'Golden Age' situated between the mythical state of nature and the social hell of eighteenth-century France; this happy state corresponded more or less to the 'primitive' societies found by the great travellers of his day – best of all, perhaps, the paradise of Tahiti reported to the French by Bougainville a few years before the *Reveries*.

Most often Rousseau's compromise was one of family life; thus the novel *Julie* includes a patriarchal idyll where a household lives in relative isolation from the wicked cities and provides a model of loving interdependence. So too, in the *Letter to D'Alembert*, there is a picture of Swiss peasant families, each living on its own plot of land and cultivating the true social virtues. What Marxists describe as Rousseau's petty-bourgeois ideal can even be glimpsed in the *Social Contract*; in spite of its reputation as a blueprint for collectivist tyranny, this work is really concerned with finding a political system which will guarantee the members of a community their individual rights and freedoms.

All of this is seen most clearly in *Émile*. Rousseau proclaims at the beginning of this book that since patriotic education is out of place in modern Europe, he is going to educate his imaginary boy as a child of nature, a self-sufficient individual. His model is Robinson Crusoe on his island – a sort of pre-figuration of the island theme in the Fifth Walk of the *Reveries*. Nevertheless, in *Émile* as in his other writings, he works towards a reconciliation of solitude and society. Robinson Crusoe returns from his island; Émile is brought up to be the natural man in society. Basically self-reliant, he learns to live with other people, to love and be loved, to contribute to the common good. At the end of the book he is married to the virtuous Sophie, and they go off to set up a virtuous patriarchal community like that of *Julie*.

It is worth noticing, however, that here as in his other writings Rousseau's imaginary state of reconciliation is only fragile. The idyll of *Julie* is destroyed, and the *Social Contract* erects an impossible model; in the *Considerations on the Government of Poland* the task of reconciling the claims of the individual and the nation is compared to squaring the circle. Even more dramatically, *Émile* has an unfinished sequel, revealingly called *The Solitaries*, which gives a fascinating preview of the mental world of the *Reveries*. Written in 1762, at a time when its author was being battered by fate, it shows Émile separated from Sophie and reduced to solitude, but learning to live from day to day and find a sort of stoical contentment in mere existence. He puts his early training in self-sufficiency to good use – but this is only a second best, and the memory of his lost happiness remains in his mind.

So too Rousseau was reduced after 1762 to finding happiness in himself, since he could not hope to realize his dreams of true friendship and social harmony. In a sense, as he says, this was a forced yet welcome return to his natural state. Yet he was never able to overcome his longing for society. Some words from the fourth book of *Émile* underline the basic and insoluble contradiction:

Every attachment is a sign of insufficiency: if each of us had no need of other people, we should scarcely think of uniting with them. Thus it is to our infirmity that we owe our fragile happiness. A truly happy being is a solitary being; only God enjoys absolute happiness, but which of us has any conception of it?

The *Reveries* is the last witness to this continuing conflict. We need only look at the passage in the Seventh Walk describing the discovery of a stocking mill and the contradictory emotions it arouses in Rousseau to see that he could never heal the breach. Repeatedly in this book he assures himself and his readers that he has at last found peace of mind in his enforced solitude, and that this was the state he was born for. Indeed the Fifth Walk evokes with great power the

'God-like' state of self-sufficient happiness hinted at in *Émile*. Yet time and again we catch a quite different note, a note of great pathos; thus in the Ninth Walk:

> Oh, if I could still enjoy some of those moments of pure and heart-felt affection, even if only from a little child, if I could still see in someone's eyes the joy and satisfaction of being with me, how these brief but happy effusions of the heart would compensate me for my many troubles and afflictions! No longer should I have to seek among animals the kind looks that humanity now refuses me!

Or in the First Walk, in baffled wonderment:

> After the fifteen years or more that this strange state of affairs has lasted, I still imagine that I am suffering from indigestion and dreaming a bad dream, from which I shall wake with my pain gone to find myself once again in the midst of my friends.

Rousseau may have been deluded and extravagant, but it is hard not to be moved by his complaints.

Nearly a century later, the predicament of the Solitary Walker is mockingly and tragically echoed in Dostoyevsky's Underground Man, who flaunts a loneliness which is partly forced upon him and partly self-imposed, but whose sense of loss and longing for real human society is apparent in all he does. And of course these have become depressingly familiar notes in modern literature, with its isolated heroes and heroines and its degraded communities. Rousseau was one of the first great writers to feel and express this agony in all its force, and he wrote memorably of the difficulty of living either alone or with others, the rejection of an unsatisfactory society and the contradictory demand or longing for the true society that he glimpsed or imagined and for the solitary happiness he had known on the Island of Saint-Pierre. One may well reject these demands or dreams as fantastic, unattainable and even dangerous. Nor is it difficult to brand their author as self-deluding and self-righteous. But in my view he continues to speak from two hundred years ago with a power and immediacy that you will hardly find in any of his contemporaries.

*

This volume is, as far as I know, the third English translation of the *Reveries*. The first was printed alongside the first part of the *Confessions* in the English edition of 1783 and does not seem to have met with much success; the translator's name is not given. The second was the work of John Gould Fletcher. It was published in London in 1927 and has been reprinted once in America. As well as what seems to me a rather arrogant introduction, it contains a good many mistakes and over-literal renderings, and in any case it is now very hard to come by in England. For my own translation I have used the text given by Marcel Raymond in his excellent edition for the Bibliothèque de la Pléiade. Following his indications, I have tried to keep as much as possible of the original punctuation; Rousseau attached a great deal of importance to the rhythm of his sentences, which can be spoiled by excessively heavy, grammatical punctuation. I have done what I can to render something of the music and eloquence which brought Rousseau so many enthusiastic readers in his time. Times have changed of course, and standards of eloquence with them, but the *Reveries* was not written in the late twentieth century, and if its author speaks strongly to us now, it is from another age and in a style which is no longer ours. Like all translators I have made compromises, but I believe that in a book such as this the manner is a part of the matter. Rousseau is as he writes.

Finally, let me thank my wife Siân for her criticisms and suggestions, and also Professor Ian Donaldson and the Humanities Research Centre of the Australian National University in Canberra for their hospitality during the summer (or rather Australian winter) of 1977 when I was working on this translation.

A BRIEF CHRONOLOGY

28 June 1712 Jean-Jacques Rousseau born in Geneva. His mother dies a few days later.

1722 Father goes into voluntary exile after a fight.

1724–8 Apprenticed to a lawyer, then to an engraver.

1728 Leaves Geneva. First meeting with Madame de Warens. Becomes a Catholic convert in Turin.

1728–31 Wandering and a variety of jobs in Italy, Switzerland and France.

1731–40 Lives mainly in or near Chambéry, protected by Madame de Warens, who becomes his mistress in 1733. Many different occupations, notably music-teaching and an extensive course of reading.

1740–41 Tutor at Lyon.

1742 Settles in Paris. Unsuccessful presentation of a new system of musical notation to the Academy of Sciences.

1743–4 Secretary to the French Ambassador in Venice.

1744 Beginning of his liaison with Thérèse Levasseur.

1744–51 Makes a living as secretary, tutor and musician, protected by the Dupin family. Collaborates on the *Encyclopedia* and frequents Diderot, Condillac and other young men of letters.

1751 Publication of the *Discourse on the Sciences and the Arts*. Beginning of Rousseau's 'reform'.

1752 Successful performance of his opera *The Village Soothsayer*.

1754 Visits Geneva, returns to the Protestant religion.

1755 Publication of the *Discourse on Inequality*.

1756–62 Lives outside Paris in the Montmorency district, working on a series of major books.

1758 Publication of the *Letter to d'Alembert*. Break with Diderot.

1761 Publication of *Julie* (*La Nouvelle Héloïse*).

1762 Publication of *Émile* and *The Social Contract*. Leaves France to avoid arrest.

1762–5 Lives in the region of Neuchâtel. Engaged in polemic caused by *Émile* and *The Social Contract*.

1763 Renounces Genevan citizenship.

1765 Driven from his home at Môtiers, takes refuge on the Island of Saint-Pierre.

1766–7 Takes refuge in England.

1766–70 Composition of the *Confessions*.

1767–70 Lives successively at various places in the French provinces.

1770 Settles again in Paris.

1771–2 Composition of *Considerations on the Government of Poland*.

1771–3 Composition of *Letters on Botany*.

1772–6 Composition of the *Dialogues* (*Rousseau, the Judge of Jean-Jacques*).

1776–8 Composition of the *Reveries*.

1778 Moves to Ermenonville.

2 July 1778 Dies at Ermenonville.

It should be remembered that in spite of the efforts of a host of scholars, there are still many gaps in our knowledge of Rousseau's life, particularly the early years. To give just one example, many people have doubted whether he did in fact have any children by Thérèse Levasseur, let alone place them in the Foundlings' Home.

FIRST WALK

You must accept humanity with all its frailty to have friends

So now I am alone in the world, with no brother, neighbour or friend, nor any company left me but my own. The most sociable and loving of men has with one accord been cast out by all the rest. With all the ingenuity of hate they have sought out the cruellest torture for my sensitive soul, and have violently broken all the threads that bound me to them. I would have loved my fellow-men in spite of themselves. It was only by ceasing to be human that they could forfeit my affection. So now they are strangers and foreigners to me; they no longer exist for me, since such is their will. But I, detached as I am from them and from the whole world, what am I? This must now be the object of my inquiry. Unfortunately, before setting out on this quest, I must glance rapidly at my present situation, for this is a necessary stage on the road that leads from them to myself.

After the fifteen years or more that this strange state of affairs has lasted, I still imagine that I am suffering from indigestion and dreaming a bad dream, from which I shall wake with my pain gone to find myself once again in the midst of my friends. Yes, I must surely have slipped unwittingly from waking into sleep, or rather from life into death. Wrenched somehow out of the natural order, I have been plunged into an incomprehensible chaos where I can make nothing out, and the more I think about my present situation, the less I can understand what has become of me.

How indeed could I ever have foreseen the fate that lay in wait for me? How can I envisage it even today, when I have succumbed to it? Could I, in my right mind, suppose that I, the very same man who I was then and am still today, would be taken beyond all doubt for a monster, a poisoner, an assassin, that I would become the horror of the human race, the laughing-stock of the rabble, that all the recognition I would receive from passers-by would be to be spat upon, and that an entire generation would of one accord take pleasure in burying me alive? At the time of this amazing transformation, my instinctive reaction was one of consternation. My emotion and indignation plunged me into a fever which has taken all of ten years to abate, and during this time, as I lurched from fault to fault, error to error, and folly to folly, my imprudent behaviour provided those who control my fate with weapons which they have most skilfully used to settle my destiny irrevocably.

For a long time I put up a resistance as violent as it was fruitless. Being without guile, without skill, without cunning and without prudence, frank, open, impatient and impulsive, I only enmeshed myself further in my efforts to be free, and constantly gave them new holds on me which they took good care not to neglect. But realizing eventually that all my efforts were in vain and my self-torment of no avail, I took the only course left to me, that of submitting to my fate and ceasing to fight against the inevitable. This resignation has made up for all my trials by the peace of mind it brings me, a peace of mind incompatible with the unceasing exertions of a struggle as painful as it was unavailing.

One other thing has contributed to this peaceful state of mind. In all the ingenuity of their hate, my persecutors were led by their animosity to overlook one detail; they forgot the need for a gradation of effects which would have allowed them to be constantly reviving and renewing my pain with some new torment. If they had been clever enough to leave me some glimmer of hope, they would still have a hold on me. They would still be able to lure me with false bait, play with me and then plunge me yet again into the torment of thwarted expectations. But they have already used every weapon at their disposal; by stripping me of everything, they have left themselves unarmed. The weight of slander, contempt, derision and opprobrium that they have heaped on me can no more be increased than it can be relieved; I am as incapable of avoiding it as they are of intensifying it. They were so eager to fill up my cup of misery that neither the power of men nor the stratagems of hell can add one drop to it. Even physical suffering would take my mind off my misfortunes rather than adding to them. Perhaps the cries of pain would save me the groans of unhappiness, and the laceration of my body would prevent that of my heart.

What have I to fear now that there is nothing more to be done? Since they can make things no worse for me, they can no longer alarm me. They have finally set me free from all the evils of anxiety and apprehension; in this at least I can find some consolation. Actual misfortunes have little effect on me; it is easy for me to accept those which I suffer in reality, but not those which I fear. My fevered imagination builds them up, works on them, magnifies them and inspects them from every angle. They are far more of a torment to me imminent than present; the threat is far worse than the blow. As soon as they happen, they lose all the terrors lent to them by imagination and appear in their true size. I find them far less formidable than I had feared, and even in the midst of my suffering I feel a sort of relief. In this state, freed from all further fear and from the anxieties of hope, I shall learn from mere habit to accept ever more easily a situation which can grow no worse; and as my awareness of it is dulled by time they can find no further way of reviving it. So much good my persecutors have done me by recklessly pouring out all the shafts of their hatred. They have deprived themselves of any power over me and henceforward I can laugh at them.

It is not yet two months since a total calm returned to my heart. I had long been without fear, but I continued to hope, and this hope, being alternately encouraged and dashed, was a hold by which a thousand different passions kept me in a state of constant agitation. A recent event as sad as it was unexpected has finally extinguished this feeble ray of hope and shown me that my earthly destiny is irrevocably fixed for all time. Since then I have resigned myself utterly and recovered my peace of mind.

As soon as I began to glimpse the plot in all its ramifications, I lost for ever all notions of changing the public's idea of me during my lifetime; indeed such a change would in future be useless to me since it could no longer be reciprocal. My fellow-men might return to me, but I should no longer be there to meet them. Such is the disdain they have inspired in me that I should find their company tedious and even burdensome, and I am a hundred times happier in my solitude than I could be if I lived among them. They have torn from my heart all the pleasures of society. These can no longer spring up again at my age; it is too late. Let them henceforth do me good or evil, all their actions are indifferent to me, and whatever they may do, my contemporaries will always be as nothing in my eyes.

But I was still counting on the future, and I hoped that a better generation, examining more closely both the judgement pronounced against me by the present generation and its conduct towards me, would find it easy to unravel the stratagems of those who control it and would at last see me as I really am. This was the hope that made me write my *Dialogues* and inspired me with a host of crazy schemes to transmit them to posterity. This hope, distant as it was, kept my soul in the same agitated state as when I was still in search of one just man in the present age, and even if I projected my dreams far into the future, they made me no less a plaything of the men of today. I have explained in the *Dialogues* on what I based this hope. I was mistaken. Fortunately I have

realized this soon enough to enjoy before I die a brief period
of complete calm and absolute tranquillity. This period began
at the time I have mentioned and I have reason to believe that
it will continue without interruption.

Hardly a day passes without some new reflections which
impress on me how wrong I was to expect the public to
change its mind about me even in some future age, since it is
guided in its behaviour towards me by mentors who constantly succeed one another in the corporations which have
come to hate me. Individuals may die, but not corporate
bodies. The same passions live on and their violent hatred, as
immortal as the demon that inspires it, remains as active as
ever. When all my individual enemies are dead there will still
be the doctors and Oratorians,[1] and even if these two bodies
were my only persecutors, I can be sure that they would no
more leave my memory in peace when I die than my person
when I am alive. Perhaps with the passage of time the doctors,
whom I really did offend, will relent, but the Oratorians, whom
I loved, honoured, trusted and never offended, the Oratorians,
who are churchmen and well-nigh monks, will remain
eternally implacable; since it is their own iniquity which makes
a criminal of me, their vanity will never pardon me, and the
public, whose animosity they will assiduously keep alight,
will remain as implacable as they are.

Everything is finished for me on this earth. Neither good
nor evil can be done to me by any man. I have nothing left in
the world to fear or hope for, and this leaves me in peace at the
bottom of the abyss, a poor unfortunate mortal, but as unmoved as God himself.

Everything external is henceforth foreign to me. I no longer
have any neighbours, fellow-men or brothers in this world. I

1. Rousseau had attacked the pretensions of medicine in several works,
but it is not clear how he aroused the hostility of the religious order of
Oratorians, if indeed he did so.

REVERIES OF THE SOLITARY WALKER

live here as in some strange planet on to which I have fallen from the one I knew. All around me I can recognize nothing but objects which afflict and wound my heart, and I cannot look at anything that is close to me or round about me without discovering some subject for indignant scorn or painful emotion. Let me therefore detach my mind from these afflicting sights; they would only cause me pain, and to no end. Alone for the rest of my life, since it is only in myself that I find consolation, hope and peace of mind, my only remaining duty is towards myself and this is all I desire. This is my state of mind as I return to the rigorous and sincere self-examination that I formerly called my *Confessions*. I am devoting my last days to studying myself and preparing the account which I shall shortly have to render. Let me give myself over entirely to the pleasure of conversing with my soul, since this is the only pleasure that men cannot take away from me. If by meditating on my inner life I am able to order it better and remedy the faults that may remain there, my meditations will not be entirely in vain, and although I am now good for nothing on this earth, I shall not have totally wasted my last days. The free hours of my daily walks have often been filled with delightful contemplations which I am sorry to have forgotten. Such reflections as I have in future I shall preserve in writing; every time I read them they will recall my original pleasure. Thinking of the prize my heart deserved, I shall forget my misfortunes, my persecutors and my disgrace.

These pages will be no more than a formless record of my reveries. I myself will figure largely in them, because a solitary person inevitably thinks a lot about himself. But all the other thoughts which pass through my mind will also have their place here. I shall say what I have thought just as it came to me, with as little connection as the thoughts of this morning have with those of last night. But on the other hand I shall gain new knowledge of my nature and disposition from knowing

what feelings and thoughts nourish my mind in this strange
state. These pages may therefore be regarded as an appendix
to my *Confessions*, but I do not give them this title, for I no
longer feel that I have anything to say that could justify it.
My heart has been purified in the crucible of adversity and the
most careful self-examination can hardly find any remaining
traces of reprehensible inclinations. What could I have still
to confess when all earthly affections have been uprooted? I
have no more reason now to praise than to condemn myself:
henceforward I am of no importance among men, and this is
unavoidable since I no longer have any real relationship or
true companionship with them. No longer able to do good
which does not turn to evil, no longer able to act without
harming others or myself, my only duty now is to abstain,
and this I do with all my heart. But though my body is idle,
my mind remains active and continues to produce feelings and
thoughts, indeed its inner moral life seems to have grown
more intense with the loss of all earthly or temporal interests.
My body is now no more than an obstacle and a hindrance to
me, and I do all I can to sever my ties with it in advance.

   Such an exceptional situation is certainly worth examining
and describing, and it is to this task that I am devoting my
last days of leisure. To accomplish it successfully I ought to
proceed with order and method, but such an undertaking is
beyond me, and indeed it would divert me from my true aim,
which is to give an account of the successive variations of my
soul. I shall perform upon myself the sort of operation that
physicists conduct upon the air in order to discover its daily
fluctuations. I shall take the barometer readings of my soul,
and by doing this accurately and repeatedly I could perhaps
obtain results as reliable as theirs. However, my aim is not so
ambitious. I shall content myself with keeping a record of my
readings without trying to reduce them to a system. My
enterprise is like Montaigne's, but my motive is entirely

different, for he wrote his essays only for others to read, whereas I am writing down my reveries for myself alone. If, as I hope, I retain the same disposition of mind in my extreme old age, when the time of my departure draws near, I shall recall in reading them the pleasure I have in writing them and by thus reviving times past I shall as it were double the space of my existence. In spite of men I shall still enjoy the charms of company, and in my decrepitude I shall live with my earlier self as I might with a younger friend.

I wrote my first *Confessions* and my *Dialogues* in a continual anxiety about ways of keeping them out of the grasping hands of my persecutors and transmitting them if possible to future generations. The same anxiety no longer torments me as I write this, I know it would be useless, and the desire to be better known to men has died in my heart, leaving me profoundly indifferent to the fate both of my true writings and of the proofs of my innocence, all of which have perhaps already been destroyed for ever. Let men spy on my actions, let them be alarmed at these papers, seize them, suppress them, falsify them, from now on it is all the same to me. I neither hide them nor display them. If they are taken from me during my lifetime, I shall not lose the pleasure of having written them, nor the memory of what they contain, nor the solitary meditations which inspired them and whose source will never dry up as long as I live. If from the moment of my first disasters I had been able to refrain from resisting my fate and had taken the course I am taking now, all the efforts of men and all their terrible machinations would have left me unmoved, and they would have been no more able to disturb my tranquillity with their plotting than they can trouble it henceforth with all their victories; let them enjoy my disgrace to the full, they will not prevent me from enjoying my innocence and finishing my days peacefully in spite of them.

SECOND WALK

HAVING therefore decided to describe my habitual state of mind in this, the strangest situation which any mortal will ever know, I could think of no simpler or surer way of carrying out my plan than to keep a faithful record of my solitary walks and the reveries that occupy them, when I give free rein to my thoughts and let my ideas follow their natural course, unrestricted and unconfined. These hours of solitude and meditation are the only ones in the day when I am completely myself and my own master, with nothing to distract or hinder me, the only ones when I can truly say that I am what nature meant me to be.

I soon felt that I was undertaking this task too late in life. My imagination has lost its old power, it no longer takes fire at the contemplation of the objects that inspire it, nor does the delirium of reverie transport me as once it did. Today there is more recollection than creation in the products of my imagination, a tepid languor saps all my faculties, the vital spirit is gradually dying down within me, my soul no longer flies up without effort from its decaying prison of flesh, and were it not for the hope of a state to which I aspire because I feel that it is mine by right, I should now live only in the past. Thus if I am to contemplate myself before my decline, I must go back several years to the time when, losing all hope for this life and finding no food left on earth for my soul, I gradually learnt to feed it on its own substance and seek all its nourishment within myself.

This expedient, which I discovered all too late, proved so fertile that it was soon enough to compensate me for everything. The habit of retiring into myself eventually made me immune to the ills that beset me, and almost to the very memory of them. In this way I learnt from my own experience that the source of true happiness is within us, and that it is not in the power of men to make anyone truly miserable who is determined to be happy. For four or five years I had regularly tasted the inward joys that gentle and loving souls find in a life of contemplation. The moments of rapture and ecstasy which I sometimes experienced during these solitary walks were joys I owed to my persecutors; without them I should never have known or discovered the treasures that lay within me. Surrounded by such riches, how was I to keep a faithful record of them all? As I tried to recall so many sweet reveries, I relived them instead of describing them. The memory of this state is enough to bring it back to life; if we completely ceased to experience it, we should soon lose all knowledge of it.

I found this to be the case during the walks which followed my decision to write a sequel to my *Confessions* and particularly during the following one, in which an unforeseen accident broke the thread of my thoughts and turned them for the time being into another channel.

On Thursday, 24 October 1776, I set out after dinner along the boulevards, going as far as the Rue du Chemin-Vert,[1] which I followed to the heights of Ménilmontant; then, taking the paths across the vineyards and meadows, I crossed the charming stretch of countryside that separates Ménilmontant from Charonne; having reached this village I made a detour and returned by another path across the same fields. I was happy walking through them, feeling the same pleasure and interest that agreeable landscapes have always aroused in me,

1. This road still exists, branching off the Boulevard Beaumarchais and leading north-east across the eleventh *arrondissement* towards Ménilmontant. Much of the 'charming stretch of countryside' between Ménilmontant and Charonne is now occupied by the Père-Lachaise cemetery.

and stopping now and again to examine plants by the wayside. I noticed two which I rarely saw in the vicinity of Paris, but which were growing abundantly in this district. The first is the *picris hieracioides*, one of the Compositae, and the second the *bupleurum falcatum*, of the Umbelliferae family. This discovery delighted me and occupied my mind for a long time, until I came across a plant that is even rarer, especially on high ground, the *cerastium aquaticum*, which in spite of the accident that happened to me that same day I later found in a book I had been carrying and transferred to my collection.

Eventually, after examining in detail several other plants which I found still in flower and which in spite of their familiarity I took pleasure in seeing and enumerating, I gradually passed from these detailed observations to the equally agreeable but more affecting impressions made on me by the complete picture. The wine harvest had been completed a few days earlier, the city dwellers no longer came out this way, and the peasants too were leaving the fields until it was time for their winter work. The country was still green and pleasant, but it was deserted and many of the leaves had fallen; everything gave an impression of solitude and impending winter. This picture evoked mixed feelings of gentle sadness which were too closely akin to my age and my experience for me not to make the comparison. I saw myself at the close of an innocent and unhappy life, with a soul still full of intense feelings and a mind still adorned with a few flowers, even if they were already blighted by sadness and withered by care. Alone and neglected, I could feel the approach of the first frosts and my failing imagination no longer filled my solitude with beings formed after the desires of my heart. Sighing I said to myself: What have I done in this world? I was created to live, and I am dying without having lived. At least I am not to blame; even if I cannot offer up to my maker the good works which I was prevented from accomplishing, I can at least pay him my tribute of frustrated good intentions, of sound sentiments which were rendered ineffectual, and of a patience which was proof against the scorn of mankind. Touched by these thoughts, I retraced the history of my soul from youth to the years of maturity and then during the long period in which I have lived cut off from the society of men, the solitude in which I shall no doubt end my days. I looked back fondly on all the affections of my heart, its loving yet blind attachments, and on the ideas which had nourished my mind for the last few years, ideas more comforting than sad, and I prepared myself to recall them clearly enough to be able to describe them with a pleasure which would almost match the pleasure of experiencing them. My afternoon went by amid these peaceful meditations, and I was making my way home, very pleased with my day, when the flow of my reveries was suddenly interrupted by the event which I must now relate.

At about six in the evening I was on the hill leading down from Ménilmontant, almost opposite the Jolly Gardener, when some people walking in front of me suddenly stepped aside and I saw a Great Dane rushing at full tilt towards me, followed by a carriage. It saw me too late to be able to check its speed or change its course. I judged that my only hope of avoiding being knocked down was to leap into the air at precisely the right moment to allow the dog to pass underneath me. This lightning plan of action, which I had no time either to examine or to put into practice, was my last thought before I went down. I felt neither the impact nor my fall, nor indeed anything else until I eventually came to.

It was nearly night when I regained consciousness. I was in the arms of two or three young men who told me what had happened. The Great Dane, unable to check its onrush, had run straight into my legs and its combined mass and speed had caused me to fall forward on my face. My upper jaw, bearing the full weight of my body, had struck against the extremely

Great Dane

bumpy cobblestones, and my fall had been all the more violent because I was on a downhill slope, so that my head finished up lower than my feet. The carriage to which the dog belonged was directly behind it and would have run right over me had not the coachman instantly reined up his horses. So much I learned from those who had picked me up and were still holding me when I came to. But what I felt at that moment was too remarkable to be passed over in silence.

Night was coming on. I saw the sky, some stars, and a few leaves. This first sensation was a moment of delight. I was conscious of nothing else. In this instant I was being born again, and it seemed as if all I perceived was filled with my frail existence. Entirely taken up by the present, I could remember nothing; I had no distinct notion of myself as a person, nor had I the least idea of what had just happened to me. I did not know who I was, nor where I was; I felt neither pain, fear, nor anxiety. I watched my blood flowing as I might have watched a stream, without even thinking that the blood had anything to do with me. I felt throughout my whole being such a wonderful calm, that whenever I recall this feeling I can find nothing to compare with it in all the pleasures that stir our lives.

They asked me where I lived; I was unable to answer. I asked them where I was; they said 'at the Upper Milepost', but they might as well have said 'at Mount Atlas'. I had to ask in turn the name of the country, the town and the district where I was. Even this was not enough, it took me the whole way from there to the Boulevard to remember my address and my name. A gentleman whom I did not know, and who was kind enough to go with me some of the way, when he found that I lived at such a distance advised me to take a cab home from the Temple.[2] I was able to walk very well and

2. The old priory of the Temple was situated at the present-day Square du Temple in the third *arrondissement*.

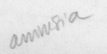
amnesia

easily, feeling no aches or cuts though I was still spitting up blood. But I was shivering with cold and this made my damaged teeth chatter most uncomfortably. When I reached the Temple, I thought that since I could walk without difficulty I would do better to continue on foot rather than run the risk of dying of cold in a cab. In this way I covered the mile or so from the Temple to the Rue Plâtrière, walking without difficulty, avoiding carriages and crowded places and picking my way as well as if I had been in perfect health. So I arrived, opened the secret lock which has been put on the street door, climbed the stairs in the dark and at length reached home with no further accident apart from my fall and its consequences – of which I was still unaware even then. My wife's cries when she saw me made me realize that I was in a worse state than I had thought. I spent the night without knowing or feeling the full extent of my injuries. In the morning I made the following painful discoveries: my upper lip was split on the inside right up to the nose; on the outside the skin had given it some protection and prevented it from coming completely apart; I had four teeth knocked in on my top jaw, all the part of my face over this jaw extremely swollen and bruised, my right thumb sprained and very swollen, my left thumb badly injured, my left arm sprained, and my left knee likewise very swollen and quite unbendable because of a violent and painful contusion. But in spite of all this battering there was nothing broken, not even a tooth – a small miracle considering what a fall I had had.

That then is a faithful account of my accident. In a matter of days the story had run through Paris, but in such an altered and distorted form as to be totally unrecognizable. I should have foreseen this metamorphosis, but it was accompanied by so many bizarre circumstances, mysterious words and silences, and told to me with such an air of absurd discretion that all this mystery began to trouble me. I have always hated darkness, it fills me naturally with a horror which has not been lessened by the gloom they have kept me plunged in for so many years now. Among the many odd events of this period I will only mention one, which will give an idea of the rest.

Monsieur Lenoir, the lieutenant-general of police, with whom I had until this time had no dealings, sent his secretary to ask after me and to make me pressing offers of favours which did not seem particularly helpful to me at this juncture. The secretary did not fail to urge me most insistently to take advantage of these offers, even going so far as to say that if I did not trust him, I could write directly to Monsieur Lenoir. This highly solicitous behaviour, together with the man's air of secrecy, showed me that there was something mysterious hidden beneath it all which I was unable to unravel. This was more than enough to upset me, particularly in the state of agitation in which my accident and the ensuing fever had left my mind. I was prey to a host of gloomy and worrying conjectures and talked about what was going on around me in a way that suggested a feverish delirium rather than the sangfroid of a man whom the world no longer interests.

Another event dealt the last blow to my peace of mind. Madame d'Ormoy had been trying to win my affection for several years without my being able to guess her reasons. Her ostentatious little presents and her frequent visits, which had no purpose and brought no pleasure, indicated clearly enough that there was a secret intention concealed here, but did not show me what it was. She had spoken to me of a novel which she wanted to write and present to the Queen. I had told her what I thought of women authors. She had given me to understand that this plan of hers was intended to restore her fortune, since this could not be done without a protector; I could answer nothing to that. Later she told me that not being able to reach the Queen, she had decided to offer her book to the public. There was no longer any point in giving her advice which was not wanted and would not have been followed in any case. She had talked about showing me her manuscript in advance. I begged her to do nothing of the kind – and she did nothing of the kind.

One fine day during my convalescence I received the novel from her all printed and even bound, and I found in the preface such exaggerated praise of me, so out of place, vulgar and affected, that it made an unpleasant impression on me. This sort of crude flattery is never the work of true benevolence, and my heart could never be deceived in such a matter.

A few days later Madame d'Ormoy came to see me with her daughter. She told me that her book was causing a sensation because of one of the footnotes which I had hardly noticed when skimming through the novel. I reread it when she had gone, looked carefully at the way it was phrased, and finally felt convinced that all her visits and blandishments and all the crude praise in her preface had had no other aim than to lead the public into attributing this note to me and loading on to me the blame which its author rightly deserved for publishing it in these circumstances.[3]

I had no way of scotching this rumour and the impression which it might create; all I could do was not to encourage it by allowing Madame d'Ormoy and her daughter to continue their unnecessary and ostentatious visits. To this end I wrote the mother the following note: 'Rousseau thanks Madame d'Ormoy for her kindnesses, but regrets that since he receives no authors he must request her not to honour him with any further visits.'

She replied with a letter which was to all appearances unexceptionable, but written in just the same way as all the

3. There is a censored passage in Madame d'Ormoy's novel *Les Malheurs de la jeune Émilie* which may be what Rousseau has in mind. It criticizes monarchs who neglect their people's welfare.

others I receive in similar circumstances. I had barbarously plunged a dagger into her tender heart, and the tone of her letter would show me that since her feelings for me were so strong and sincere she could not hope to survive this break. So it is that all kinds of frankness and honesty are terrible crimes in the eyes of society; I should seem wicked and ferocious to my contemporaries even if my only crime lay in not being as false and perfidious as they are.

I had already gone out several times and was even taking quite frequent walks in the Tuileries, when I saw from the astonishment of many of those whom I met that there was some other story about me that I had not yet heard. Finally I learned that I was rumoured to have died from my fall, and this rumour had spread so quickly and irresistibly that more than two weeks after I heard it the King himself and the Queen were talking as if there were no doubt about it. The *Courrier* of Avignon, as they took care to inform me, not only announced this happy event, but did not fail to provide a foretaste of the tribute of insults and indignities which are being prepared to honour my memory by way of a funeral oration.[4]

This piece of news was accompanied by one even more curious circumstance; I only learned of this by chance, and was unable to discover any details. It was that a subscription had been opened at the same time for printing any manuscripts that were found in my apartment. This showed me that they had a collection of specially fabricated works ready to be attributed to me as soon as I was dead, for the idea that they would faithfully reproduce anything that I might really

4. The obituary notice in the Avignon *Courrier* says among other things: 'We are sorry not to be able to speak of the talents of this eloquent writer; our readers will no doubt feel that his abuse of them imposes the strictest silence on us.'

leave was a piece of folly that no sensible man could entertain and that the experience of fifteen years has been more than enough to guard me against.

These observations, coming one after another and followed by many more which were almost equally astonishing, caused a renewed alarm in my imagination, which I had thought was deadened; and these black shadows which they were constantly piling up around me revived all the horror that darkness naturally provokes in me. I wore myself out finding endless explanations for all this and trying to understand mysteries which have been made deliberately unintelligible to me. The one unchanging solution to all these riddles was the confirmation of all my previous conclusions, namely that since my fate and the fate of my reputation had been decided in advance by the concerted efforts of the present generation, no effort on my part could save me from it, for I can have no chance of handing on anything precious to future ages without its passing through hands that have an interest in suppressing it.

But on this occasion I went one step further. The accumulation of so many chance circumstances, the elevation of all my cruellest enemies, as if chosen by fortune, the way in which all those who govern the nation or control public opinion, all those who occupy places of credit and authority seem to have been hand-picked from among those who harbour some secret animosity towards me to take part in the universal conspiracy, all this is too extraordinary to be a mere coincidence. In order for it to fail, all that was needed was one refusal to be an accomplice, one contrary turn of events, one unexpected circumstance which got in its way. But every individual will, every turn of fate, every change in fortune, has served to consolidate this work of men's hands, and such a striking and incredible combination of circumstances leaves me in no doubt that it is Heaven's eternal decree that their designs shall be crowned with complete success. A host of detailed observations both in the present and in the past affords such total confirmation of this conclusion of mine that henceforward I cannot help regarding as a divine secret beyond the reach of human reason the plot that I previously saw as nothing but the fruit of human malevolence.

This idea, so far from seeming cruel or unbearable, brings me consolation, tranquillity and resignation. I do not go so far as Saint Augustine, who would have been content to be damned if such had been the will of God. My resignation is of a less disinterested kind perhaps, but its origin is no less pure and I believe it is more worthy of the perfect Being whom I adore.

God is just; his will is that I should suffer, and he knows my innocence. That is what gives me confidence. My heart and my reason cry out that I shall not be disappointed. Let men and fate do their worst, we must learn to suffer in silence, everything will find its proper place in the end and sooner or later my turn will come.

persecuted
paranoid – I
have met people
like this in
coffeeshops

THIRD WALK

Growing older, I learn all the time.

Solon often repeated this line in his old age. In a sense I could say the same, but the knowledge that the experience of twenty years has brought me is a poor thing, and even ignorance would be preferable. No doubt adversity is a great teacher, but its lessons are dearly bought, and often the profit we gain from them is not worth the price they cost us. What is more, these lessons come so late in the day that by the time we master them they are of no use to us. Youth is the time to study wisdom, age the time to practise it. Experience is always instructive, I admit, but it is only useful in the time we have left to live. When death is already at the door, is it worth learning how we should have lived?

What use to me are the insights I have gained so late and so painfully into my destiny and the passions of those who have made it what it is? If I have learned to know men better, it is only to feel more keenly the misery into which they have plunged me, nor has this knowledge, while laying bare all their traps, enabled me to avoid a single one. Why did I not remain in that foolish yet blessed faith, which made me for so many years the prey and plaything of my vociferous friends with never the least suspicion of all the plots enveloping me. I was their dupe and their victim, to be sure, but I believed they loved me, my heart enjoyed the friendship they had inspired in me, and I credited them with the same feelings. Those sweet illusions have been destroyed. The sad truth that time and reason have revealed to me in making me aware of my misfortune, has convinced me that there is no remedy and that resignation is my only course. Thus all the experience of

47

my old age is of no use to me in my present state, nor will it help me in the future.

We enter the race when we are born and we leave it when we die. Why learn to drive your chariot better when you are close to the finishing post? All you have to consider then is how to make your exit. If an old man has something to learn, it is the art of dying, and this is precisely what occupies people least at my age; we think of anything rather than that. Old men are all more attached to life than children, and they leave it with a worse grace than the young. This is because all their labours have had this life in view, and at the end they see that it has all been in vain. When they go, they leave everything behind, all their concerns, all their goods, and the fruits of all their tireless endeavours. They have not thought to acquire anything during their lives that they could take with them when they die.

I told myself all this when there was still time, and if I have not been able to make better use of my reflections, this is not because they came too late or remained undigested. Thrown into the whirlpool of life while still a child, I learned from early experience that I was not made for this world, and that in it I would never attain the state to which my heart aspired. Ceasing therefore to seek among men the happiness which I felt I could never find there, my ardent imagination learned to leap over the boundaries of a life which was as yet hardly begun, as if it were flying over an alien land in search of a fixed and stable resting-place.

This desire, fostered by my early education and later strengthened by the long train of miseries and misfortunes that have filled my life, has at all times led me to seek after the nature and purpose of my being with greater interest and determination than I have seen in anyone else. I have met many men who were more learned in their philosophizing, but their philosophy remained as it were external to them. Wishing to know more than other people, they studied the workings of the universe, as they might have studied some machine they had come across, out of sheer curiosity. They studied human nature in order to speak knowledgeably about it, not in order to know themselves; their efforts were directed to the instruction of others and not to their own inner enlightenment. Several of them merely wanted to write a book, any book, so long as it was successful. Once it was written and published, its contents no longer interested them in the least. All they wanted was to have it accepted by other people and to defend it when it was attacked; beyond this they neither took anything from it for their own use nor concerned themselves with its truth or falsehood, provided it escaped refutation. For my part, when I have set out to learn something, my aim has been to gain knowledge for myself and not to be a teacher; I have always thought that before instructing others one should begin by knowing enough for one's own needs, and of all the studies I have undertaken in my life among men, there is hardly one that I would not equally have undertaken if I had been confined to a desert island for the rest of my days. What we ought to do depends largely on what we ought to believe, and in all matters other than the basic needs of our nature our opinions govern our actions. This principle, to which I have always adhered, has frequently led me to seek at length for the true purpose of my life so as to be able to determine its conduct, and feeling that this purpose was not to be found among men, I soon became reconciled to my incapacity for worldly success.

Born into a moral and pious family and brought up affectionately by a minister full of virtue and religion, I had received from my earliest years principles and maxims – prejudices, some might say – which have never entirely deserted me. While I was still a child, left to my own devices, led on by kindness, seduced by vanity, duped by hope and compelled by necessity, I became a Catholic, but I remained a Christian and soon my heart, under the influence of habit, became sincerely attached to my new religion. The instruction and good example I received from Madame de Warens confirmed me in this attachment. The rural solitude in which I spent the best days of my youth, and the reading of good books which completely absorbed me, strengthened my naturally affectionate tendencies in her company and led me to an almost Fénelon-like devotion. Lonely meditation, the study of nature and the contemplation of the universe lead the solitary to aspire continually to the maker of all things and to seek with a pleasing disquiet for the purpose of all he sees and the cause of all he feels. When my destiny cast me back into the torrent of this world, I found nothing there which could satisfy my heart for a single moment. Regret for the sweet liberty I had lost followed me everywhere and threw a veil of indifference or distaste over everything around me which might have brought me fame and fortune. Wavering in my uncertain desires, I hoped for little and obtained less, and even amidst the gleams of prosperity that came my way I felt that had I obtained all I thought I wanted, it would not have given me the happiness that my heart thirsted after without knowing clearly what it was. In this way everything conspired to detach my affections from this world, even before the onset of those misfortunes which were to make me a total stranger to it. I reached the age of forty, oscillating between poverty and riches, wisdom and error, full of vices born of habit, but with a heart free of evil inclinations, living at random with no rational principles, and careless but not scornful of my duties, of which I was often not fully aware.

Since the days of my youth I had fixed on the age of forty as the end of my efforts to succeed, the final term of my various ambitions. I had the firm intention, when I reached this age, of making no further effort to climb out of whatever situation I was in and of spending the rest of my life living from day to day with no thought for the future. When the time came I carried out my plan without difficulty, and although my fortune at that time seemed to be on the point of changing permanently for the better,[1] it was not only without regret but with real pleasure that I gave up these prospects. In shaking off all these lures and vain hopes, I abandoned myself entirely to the nonchalant tranquillity which has always been my dominant taste and most lasting inclination. I quitted the world and its vanities, I gave up all finery – no more sword, no more watch, no more white stockings, gilt trimmings and powder, but a simple wig and a good solid coat of broadcloth – and what is more than all the rest, I uprooted from my heart the greed and covetousness which give value to all I was leaving behind. I gave up the position I was then occupying, a position for which I was quite unsuited, and set myself to copying music at so much a page, an occupation for which I had always had a distinct liking.

I did not confine my reformation to outward things. Indeed I became aware that this change called for a revision of my opinions, which although undoubtedly more painful was also more necessary, and resolving to get it all over at once, I set about a strict self-examination which was to order my inner life for the rest of my days as I would wish it to be at the time of my death.

A great change which had recently come over me, a new moral vision of the world which had opened before me, the foolish judgements of men, whose absurdity I was beginning to sense without foreseeing how I was to fall victim to them, the ever-growing desire for something other than the literary celebrity which had hardly reached my nostrils before I was

1. In 1751, at the time of the success of the *Discourse on the Sciences and the Arts*, Rousseau was given the lucrative post of cashier by his patron Francueil, who was Receiver-General of Finances. He very soon resigned it.

of it, and finally the wish to find a less uncertain
the rest of my career than that in which I had already
the better half of it, all this impressed on me the long-
need for such a general review of my opinions. I under-
took it therefore, and neglected nothing in my power to carry
it out successfully.

It is from this time that I can date my total renunciation of
the world and the great love of solitude which has never since
left me. The task I had set myself could only be performed in
absolute isolation; it called for long and tranquil meditations
which are impossible in the bustle of society life. So I was
obliged to adopt for a time another way of life, which I subsequently found so much to my taste that since then I have
only interrupted it for brief periods and against my will, returning to it most gladly and following it without effort as
soon as I was able; and when men later reduced me to a life
of solitude, I found that in isolating me to make me miserable, they had done more for my happiness than I had been
able to do myself.

I set about the task I had undertaken with a zeal proportionate to the importance of the subject and its value to me. At
this time I was living among certain modern philosophers who
had little in common with the philosophers of antiquity.
Instead of removing my doubts and curing my uncertainties
they had shaken all my most assured beliefs concerning the
questions which were most important to me, for these ardent
missionaries of atheism, these overbearing dogmatists could
not patiently endure that anyone should think differently
from them on any subject whatsoever. I often defended myself
rather feebly because of my distaste and lack of talent for
disputation, but never once did I adopt their dismal teaching,
and this resistance to such intolerant people, who had moreover their own ends in view, was not the least of the causes
which sparked off their animosity towards me.

They had not persuaded me, but they had troubled me.
Their arguments had shaken me without ever convincing me;
I could not find the real answer to what they said, but I felt
sure there must be one. I charged myself not so much with
being mistaken as with being incompetent, and my heart
answered them better than my reason.

Finally I said to myself: 'Shall I allow myself to be tossed
eternally to and fro by the sophistries of the eloquent, when I
am not even sure that the opinions they preach and press so
ardently on others are really their own? Their passions, which
determine their doctrine, and their interest in having this or
that belief accepted, make it impossible to know what they
themselves believe. Can one expect good faith from the
leaders of parties? Their philosophy is meant for others; I
need one for myself. Let me seek it with all my might while
there is still time, so that I may have an assured rule of conduct
for the rest of my days. I am now in the prime of life and the
fullness of my mental powers. I am about to enter my decline.
If I wait any longer, I shall no longer have all my powers to
devote to my tardy deliberations, my intellectual faculties will
have lost some of their vigour and I shall then do less well
what today I can do as well as I ever shall; let me seize on this
auspicious moment; it is the time of my outward and material
reformation, let it also be the time of my intellectual and
moral reformation. Let me decide my opinions and principles
once and for all, and then let me remain for the rest of my life
what mature consideration tells me I should be.'

I put this plan into effect slowly and haltingly, but I devoted
to it all the effort and attention of which I was capable. I felt
keenly that the tranquillity of the rest of my life and indeed
my whole destiny depended on it. At the outset I found myself
plunged into such a labyrinth of problems, difficulties,
objections, complexities and obscurities that I was repeatedly
tempted to abandon everything and was on the point of giving

up my fruitless research and relying on the rules of common prudence in my deliberations without trying any further to find new rules in the principles which I had such difficulty in disentangling. But this prudence was itself so foreign to me and I felt so incapable of attaining it, that to take it for my guide would have been like searching through high seas and storms, without helm or compass, for a scarcely visible lantern which could never light my way to any port.

I persevered: for the first time in my life I acted courageously, and it is thanks to this success that I was able to withstand the horrible fate which was then beginning to envelop me without my having the least suspicion of it. After what were perhaps the most ardent and sincere investigations ever conducted by any mortal, I made up my mind once and for all on all the questions that concerned me, and if I was mistaken in my conclusions, I am sure at least that I cannot be blamed for my error since I did all I could to avoid it. It is true no doubt that the prejudices of childhood and the secret wishes of my heart tipped the scales on the side which was most comforting to me. It is hard to prevent oneself from believing what one so keenly desires, and who can doubt that the interest we have in admitting or denying the reality of the Judgement to come determines the faith of most men in accordance with their hopes and fears. All this may have led my reason astray, I admit, but it could not affect my good faith, for I was constantly in fear of error. If the use we made of this life was all that mattered, then it was important that I should know it, so as to be able to make the most of it while I still had time and not be a complete dupe. But what I feared most in the mood I was in, was to endanger the eternal fate of my soul for the sake of those worldly pleasures which have never seemed very precious to me.

I confess too that I did not always resolve to my own satisfaction all the difficulties which had perplexed me and which our philosophers had so often drummed into my ears. But having determined to make a final decision on matters which are so baffling to the human mind, and finding on all sides impenetrable mysteries and unanswerable objections, I adopted in every case the opinion which seemed to me the most clearly proved and the most credible in itself, without worrying about objections which I could not resolve, but which were met by other equally powerful objections in the opposing system. Only a charlatan will be dogmatic on such questions, but we must all have our own opinion and must choose it with all the maturity of judgement of which we are capable. If in spite of this we still fall into error, we cannot in justice be held responsible for it, since we are not to blame. This is the unshakable principle on which I base my confidence.

The result of my arduous research was more or less what I have written down in my 'Profession of Faith of a Savoyard Priest', a work which has been ignobly prostituted and desecrated by the present generation, but which may one day effect a revolution in the minds of men, if ever good sense and good faith return among them.[2]

Since then, remaining steadfast in the principles which I adopted after such long and careful meditation, I have made them the constant rule of my belief and conduct without wasting any further thought on the objections which I was unable to answer or on those which I had not foreseen and which arose from time to time in my mind. Sometimes they have worried me, but they have never shaken my faith. I have always said to myself: 'All these are hair-splitting metaphysical subtleties which count for nothing against the basic

2. This 'Profession of Faith' is included in Book 4 of the treatise on education, *Émile*. Arguing for a theistic natural religion and containing vigorous criticisms of orthodox Catholicism, it was largely responsible for the severe measures taken against Rousseau in 1762 by the French authorities.

principles adopted by my reason, confirmed by my heart and bearing the seal of my conscience uninfluenced by passion. In matters so far above human understanding, shall I let an objection that I cannot answer overturn a whole body of doctrine which is so sound and coherent, the result of so much careful meditation, so well fitted to my reason, my heart and my whole being, and confirmed by that inner voice that I find absent from all the rest? No, empty logic-chopping will never destroy the close relation I perceive between my immortal nature and the constitution of the world, the physical order I see all around me. In the corresponding moral order, which my researches have brought to light, I find the support I need to be able to endure the miseries of my life. In any other system I should have no resources for living and no hope when dying. I should be the most unfortunate of creatures. Let us hold fast then to the only system which is able to make me happy in spite of fortune and my fellow-men.'

Do not these reflections and the conclusion I drew from them seem to have been sent down by Heaven itself to prepare me for the fate that awaited me and enable me to endure it? What would have become of me, what would become of me even now, in the terrible anguish that awaited me and in the unbelievable situation to which I am reduced for the rest of my days if, deprived of a refuge from my implacable persecutors, a consolation for the ignominy they force me to endure in this world, and a hope of obtaining one day the justice that is due to me, I had been abandoned entirely to the most horrible fate that a mortal has ever suffered on this earth? All the time when, untroubled in my innocence, I imagined that men felt nothing but benevolence and respect towards me and opened my frank and trusting heart to my friends and brothers, the traitors were silently ensnaring me in traps forged in the depths of hell. Taken unawares by this most unforeseen of misfortunes, the most terrible there is for a proud soul, tram-

pled in the mire without knowing why or by whom, dragged
into a pit of ignominy, enveloped in a horrible darkness
through which I could make out nothing but sinister appari-
tions, I was overwhelmed by the first shock, and I should
never have recovered from the prostration into which I was
cast by the unexpectedness of this castrophe, if I had not previously prepared the support I needed to struggle to my feet
again.

It was only after years of anxiety, when I finally pulled
myself together and began to be myself again, that I felt the
value of the resources I had made ready against adversity.
Having made up my mind on every question that concerned
me, I saw, when I set my principles against the situation I was
in, that I was giving far more than their real importance to the
senseless judgements of men and the petty events of this brief
life, that this life being merely a testing time, it mattered little
what particular form of ordeal one encountered so long as the
result was as it should be, and that therefore the greater, the
more testing and the more numerous the ordeals, the more
deserving it was to be able to endure them. All the sharpest
torments lose their sting if one can confidently expect a
glorious recompense, and the certainty of this recompense
was the principal fruit of my earlier meditations.

It is true that in the midst of the unnumerable injuries and
monstrous humiliations which were heaped on me from all
sides, there were moments of doubt and anxiety when my
faith was shaken and my peace disturbed. At such times the
powerful objections which I had not been able to answer
confronted my mind with renewed force and dealt me a final
blow at precisely the moment when, overburdened by the
weight of my destiny, I was on the point of giving way to
discouragement. New arguments I heard would often return
to reinforce those which had already tormented me. Then I
would say to myself, my heart nearly bursting with agony:

'Oh, who can protect me from despair if in the horror of my fate I see nothing but fantasies in the consolation offered me by my own reason, if it can thus destroy its own work and overturn the edifice of hope and faith that it had built up in adversity! What help can I receive from illusions which deceive no one but me? The people of today see nothing but error and prejudice in the opinions in which I alone seek sustenance; in their eyes the truth is to be found in the system opposed to mine; they do not even seem able to believe that I have adopted mine in good faith, and I myself, even when I give myself over whole-heartedly to this faith, am faced by insurmountable difficulties that I cannot resolve. Yet I continue to believe in spite of them. Am I then the only wise man, the only man who has seen the light? Can I believe in an order of things simply because it suits me? Can I put an enlightened trust in appearances which lack all solidity in the eyes of my contemporaries and would seem illusory to me if my reason were not supported by my heart? Would it not have been better to combat my persecutors with their own weapons, adopting their principles rather than clinging to my own illusions, which I cannot defend against their onslaught? I think myself wise, but I am a mere dupe, a victim and a martyr to an empty illusion.'

How often in these moments of doubt and uncertainty I was on the point of giving way to despair! If ever I had spent a whole month in this state, it would have been the end of me. But these crises, although once quite frequent, were always short-lived, and now, when I am still not quite free of them, they are so brief and infrequent that they have not even the power to disturb my peace of mind. They are mere flickers of anxiety which have no more effect on my soul than a feather falling into the water can have on the course of a river. I have realized that to raise again the points on which I had already made up my mind was to imagine that I had new insights or a better judgement or a greater desire for truth than at the time of my researches, and that since none of these was or could be the case with me, I could have no sound reason for preferring opinions which only tempted me so as to aggravate my unhappy state of despair, to opinions which I had adopted in the prime of life and the fullness of my mental powers, after the most profound consideration, and at a time when my untroubled life left me with no dominant interest other than that of discovering the truth. Today, when my heart is torn by anguish, my soul borne down by misery, my imagination clouded by fear and my head troubled by all the terrible mysteries that surround me, today when all my faculties have been enfeebled by age and care, shall I light-heartedly deprive myself of all the resources I had stored up for myself and place more trust in my declining reason, which makes me unjustly miserable, than in my mature and vigorous reason, which offers me a compensation for all my undeserved suffering?

No, I am neither wiser, nor better informed, nor more sincere than when I made up my mind on these important matters; I was well aware then of the objections which I allow to worry me today; they did not deter me then, and if some new and unforeseen difficulties have arisen, they are only the subtle sophistries of metaphysicians and cannot outweigh the eternal truths which have been accepted at all times and by all wise men, recognized by all nations, and indelibly engraved on the human heart. I knew, when I was pondering these things, that the human understanding, limited by the senses, could not fully comprehend them. I confined myself therefore to what was within my reach and did not attempt to understand what was beyond me. This was a reasonable course of action, I adopted it in the past and kept to it with the approval of my heart and my reason. What cause have I to abandon it at a time when so many powerful motives impel me to continue in it? What danger is there in following it? What would I gain from changing course? If I were to adopt the teaching of my persecutors, should I also adopt their morality – the rootless and sterile morality which they expound so grandiloquently in their books or with bravado in their plays but which never makes its way to the heart or the reason, or else the cruel secret morality, for which the other is only a mask, the esoteric doctrine of all their initiates which governs their behaviour and which they have so cleverly exercised at my expense? This morality is purely offensive, useless for self-defence and only good for attack. What use would it be to me in the state to which they have reduced me? Only my innocence gives me strength in my misfortunes; how much more miserable I should be if I deprived myself of this single but powerful support and put malice in its place! Should I equal them in the art of mischief, and if I did, how would the harm I did them help me? I should lose my own self-respect and gain nothing in its place.

In this way, reasoning with myself, I was able to preserve my principles unshaken by specious arguments, insoluble objections and difficulties which lay beyond my reach and perhaps beyond that of the human mind. My own mind, resting on the most solid foundations I was able to provide, became so used to remaining there in the shelter of my conscience that no strange doctrine, old or new, can any longer disturb my peace for a single moment. Sunk in mental lethargy, I have forgotten the very arguments on which I based my belief and my principles, but I shall never forget the conclusions I drew from them with the approval of my conscience and my reason, and henceforth I shall never let them go. Let all the philosophers chop their logic against them; they will be wasting their time and their trouble. For the rest of my days I shall hold fast in all things to the position I adopted when I was better able to choose.

In this untroubled state of mind I find not only self-contentment, but the hope and consolation which my situation requires. A solitude so complete, so permanent and in itself so melancholy, the ever-present and constantly active animosity of all the present generation, the humiliations which they constantly heap on me, all this inevitably depresses me from time to time; uncertainty and worrying doubts still return occasionally to trouble my soul and fill it with gloom. Then it is that, being incapable of the thought processes which would be necessary to reassure myself, I feel the need to recall my former conclusions; I remember the painstaking attention and sincerity of heart which led me to them and all my confidence returns. Thus I reject all new ideas as fatal errors which have only a specious appearance of truth and are only fit to disturb my peace of mind.

In this way, confined to the narrow limits of my former knowledge, I have not, like Solon, the good fortune to learn all the time as I grow older, indeed I must refrain from the dangerous ambition of learning what I am no longer capable of knowing properly. But if I cannot hope to acquire much more in the way of useful knowledge, there is still much to be attained in the way of virtues necessary to my situation in life. Here it is that the time has come to enrich and adorn my soul with goods that it can carry with it when, set free of this body that obstructs and blinds it, it sees the truth face to face and comes to know the futility of all the knowledge which makes our false philosophers so vain. It will regret the moments wasted on attempts to acquire it in this life. But patience, kindness, resignation, integrity and impartial justice are goods that we can take with us and that we can accumulate continually without fear that death itself can rob us of their value. It is to this one useful study that I devote what remains of my old age. And I shall be happy if by my own self-improvement I learn to leave life, not better, for that is impossible, but more virtuous than when I entered it.

optimism & ~~that~~ taking
control of one's life & being
responsible for the improve-
ment of one's existence.
To leave not better but more
virtuous than when I had
entered it. . . .

What does
better
mean?

FOURTH WALK

AMONG the few authors whom I still read from time to time Plutarch is my favourite and the one from whom I learn the most. He was my first childhood reading and he will be the last reading of my old age; he is almost the only author whom I have never read in vain. Two days ago I was reading in his *Moralia* the essay on 'How a man may profit by his enemies'. The same day, while I was sorting out various pamphlets which had been sent me by their authors, I came across a volume of Abbé Rozier's *Journal*[1] on the title page of which he had written the words '*Vitam vero impendenti* Rozier'.[2] I was too familiar with the ways of these gentlemen to be taken in by this, and understood that this apparent compliment was meant as a cruel piece of irony. But on what grounds? Why this sarcasm? How could I have deserved it? In order to profit by the lessons of the excellent Plutarch I decided to devote my walk of the following day to a self-examination on the subject of falsehood, and I embarked on it in the firm conviction that the 'Know Thyself' of the temple at Delphi was not such an easy precept to observe as I had thought in my *Confessions*.

When I set out the next day to put this resolution into practice, my first thought on beginning to reflect was of a terrible lie I had told in my early youth, a lie the memory of which has troubled me all my life and even now, in my old age, adds sorrow to a heart already suffering in so many other

1. The official title of this periodical was *Observations sur la physique, sur l'histoire naturelle et sur les arts*.

2. Rousseau had taken as his motto Juvenal's words: '*vitam impendere vero*' – 'to devote one's life to the truth'.

ways.[3] This lie, which was a great crime in itself, was doubt-less still more evil in its effects; these have remained unknown to me, but remorse has painted them to me in the cruellest possible colours. Yet, if one were to consider only my state of mind at the time, this lie was simply the product of false shame, and far from its being the result of a desire to harm the girl who was its victim, I can swear to Heaven that at the very moment when this invincible shame dragged it from me, I would joyfully have given my life's blood to deflect the blow on to myself alone. It was a moment of irresponsible folly which I can only explain by saying what I feel to be true, that all the wishes of my heart were conquered by my innate timidity.

The memory of this deplorable act and the undying remorse it left me, instilled in me a horror of falsehood that ought to have preserved my heart from this vice for the rest of my life. When I adopted my motto, I felt that I had a right to it, and I had no doubt that I was worthy of it when I began on Abbé Rozier's prompting to examine myself more seriously.

However, on going over my life more carefully, I was very surprised by the number of things of my own invention which I remembered presenting as true at the very time when my heart was proud of my love of truth and I was sacrificing my security, my best interests and my own person to this love of truth with a disinterestedness for which I know no parallel among men.

What surprised me most was that when I recalled these fabrications I felt no real repentance. I, whose horror of false-hood outweighs all my other feelings, who would willingly face torture rather than tell a lie, by what strange inconsistency could I lie so cheerfully without compulsion or profit, and by

3. This episode is vividly described in Book 2 of the *Confessions*. While he was a servant in Turin, the young Rousseau had stolen a ribbon from his mistress and accused his fellow-servant Marion of the crime.

what incredible contradiction could I do so without the slightest twinge of regret, when remorse for a lie has continually tormented me these fifty years? I have never hardened myself against my faults; my moral sense has always been a faithful guide to me, my conscience has retained its original integrity, and even if it might be corrupted and swayed by my personal interests, how could I explain that, remaining firm and unmoved on those occasions when a man can at least excuse himself by his weakness in the face of passion, it loses its integrity precisely over those unimportant matters where vice has no excuse? I realized that the solution to this problem would determine how correctly I judged my behaviour in this respect, and after careful consideration I reached the following conclusions.

I remember reading in some philosophical work that to lie is to conceal a truth which one ought to make known. It follows of course from this definition that to conceal a truth which one is not obliged to divulge is not lying. But if in such circumstances a man not only fails to speak the truth, but speaks the opposite of the truth, is he or is he not lying? According to the definition he cannot be said to be lying. For if he gives counterfeit coin to someone to whom he owes nothing, he may indeed be a deceiver, but he is not a thief.

There are two questions to be looked at here, both of them equally important. Firstly, when and how should one tell the truth to others, since one is not always obliged to tell it? Secondly, are there cases when one can deceive people blamelessly? Of course everyone knows how to answer the second question – negatively in books, where the most austere morals cost the author nothing; affirmatively in life, where the morals of books are seen as idle and impracticable chatter. So, disregarding these conflicting authorities, let me seek by my own principles to find my answers to these questions.

In its general and abstract sense truth is the most precious of our possessions. Without it man is blind; it is the eye of reason. Through it man learns to conduct himself, to live and act as he ought, and to strive towards his true end. But in the particular or individual sense truth is not always such a good thing; sometimes it is a bad thing, and very often it is a matter of indifference. Those things which a man needs to know, and whose knowledge is necessary to his happiness, are not perhaps very numerous, but whatever their number, they are his lawful possession to which he has a right at all times, and which can only be concealed from him by the most iniquitous kind of robbery, since they are a sort of common property that can be passed on without any loss to the giver.

As for those truths which have no practical or instructive value, how could they be something that is owed to us, since they are not even a valuable possession? And since property is founded solely on usefulness, there can be no property when there is no question of use. One may lay claim to a piece of barren land, since it can at least be used as a place to live, but whether a piece of futile, unimportant and inconsequential information is true or false can be of interest to no one. There is nothing superfluous in the moral order, any more than in the physical order. Something that is good for nothing cannot be owed to anybody; for something to be owed to somebody, it must be actually or potentially useful. Thus the truth which we owe to one another is that which concerns justice, and it is a profanation of the holy name of truth to apply it to trivial things of which the existence is a matter of general indifference and the knowledge totally useless. Truth without any possible usefulness can therefore never be something we owe to one another; it follows therefore that anyone who conceals or disguises it is not telling a lie.

But are there any truths so completely sterile as to be utterly useless from every point of view? That is a different problem, injustice = harm.

to which I shall presently return. Meanwhile let us consider
the second question.

Not to say what is true and to say what is not true are two
very different things, but they can produce the same effect,
for this effect is certainly identical when it is equal to zero.
Whenever the truth is a matter of indifference, the opposite
error is a matter of equal indifference – whence it follows that
to deceive someone by speaking the opposite of the truth is no
more reprehensible than to deceive him by not speaking the
truth, since error is no worse than ignorance when the truth is
of no consequence. Whether I believe the sand at the bottom
of the sea to be red or white matters no more than if I am
ignorant of its colour. How can one be unjust if one is in-
juring no one, since injustice consists precisely in the injury
caused to others?

But these rapid answers to my questions can provide me
with no sure practical guidance unless they are accompanied
by the many preliminary glosses that are needed to apply them
correctly to every case which could arise. For if the obligation to speak the truth is founded solely on usefulness, how
can I set myself up as a judge of this usefulness? Very often one
person's gain is another's loss, and private interest is almost
always in conflict with public good. How are we to act in
such circumstances? Are we to sacrifice the interest of the
absent to that of those with whom we are speaking? Are we
or are we not to declare a truth which will favour one person
to the detriment of another? Are we to measure our obligations by the single criterion of public good or by that of
distributive justice? And can I be sure of knowing all the
aspects of a question so well that I divulge my information
purely according to the rules of equity? What is more, in
examining what one owes to others, have I taken sufficient
account of what one owes to oneself? If I do no harm to my
neighbour when I deceive him, does it follow that I do no

harm to myself, and is it enough always to avoid injustice in order to live blamelessly?

What a host of knotty problems, which it would be easy to dispose of by saying: 'Let us always act truthfully, whatever happens. Justice is inherent in truth; falsehood is always evil and error is always deceit, when we present what is not true as a rule for belief or action; and whatever truth may lead to, we are always guiltless in declaring it, since we have not added anything of our own to it.'

But this is merely to cut the Gordian knot. We were not discussing whether it would be a good thing always to tell the truth, but whether one is always equally bound to do so, and, assuming from the definition under consideration that this is not the case, how we are to distinguish between cases where the truth is absolutely required of us and those where it can be left unspoken and concealed without falsehood – for I have found that such cases do indeed exist. What we are seeking therefore is a reliable rule for knowing and determining which they are.

But where shall we find this rule, and what proof can we have of its infallibility? In all ethical questions as difficult as this I have always found it best to be guided by the voice of conscience rather than the light of reason. My moral instinct has never deceived me. It has always remained sufficiently pure within me for me to put my trust in it, and if in my conduct it is sometimes swayed by my passions, it has no difficulty in regaining its authority in my recollections. Then it is that I judge myself as severely perhaps as I shall be judged after death by the Supreme Judge.

To judge men's words by the effects they produce is often to misjudge them. Apart from the fact that these effects are not always clear or easily ascertained, they are as infinitely varied as the circumstances in which the words are spoken. But their degree of goodness or malice can only be gauged and deter-

mined by the intention that produced them. Untruthful talk
is only falsehood when deception is intended, and even the
intent to deceive, far from being invariably linked to the
desire to injure, is often produced by exactly the opposite
motive. But for falsehood to be innocent, it is not enough
that there be no deliberate harmful intent, we must also be
certain that the error into which we are leading our fellow-
men can harm neither them nor anyone else in any way whatsoever. It is only very rarely that we can attain this certainty;
consequently it is only very rarely that a lie is completely
innocent. To lie to one's own advantage is an imposture, to
lie to the advantage of others is a fraud, and to lie to the detriment of others is a slander – this is the worst kind of lie. To
lie without advantage or disadvantage to oneself or others is
not to lie; it is not falsehood but fiction.

Fictions which have a moral end in view are called parables
or fables, and since their aim is or should be to present useful
truths in a form which is pleasing to the senses, there is hardly
any attempt in such cases to conceal the factual untruth, which
is merely the disguise of truth, and the person who tells a
fable simply as a fable is not in any sense a liar.

There are also quite empty kinds of fiction, such as the
majority of stories and novels, which contain no real instruction and have no object other than entertainment. Such tales,
being without any moral value, can only be judged by the
intention of the teller, and when he tells them as if they were
actually true, it can hardly be doubted that they are in fact
lies. Even so, who has ever greatly troubled his conscience
over lies of this sort, and who has ever seriously reproached
anyone for telling them? For instance, if there is some moral
lesson in *The Temple of Gnidus*,[4] this intention is badly flawed
and obscured by the licentious details and lascivious images of
the book. What did the author do to spread a cloak of modesty

4. A story by Montesquieu, published in 1725.

69

over his work? He pretended that it was the translation of a Greek manuscript and described the discovery of this manuscript in the manner most calculated to persuade his readers of the truth of his account. If that is not positively a lie, I should like to know what the word means. Yet who has ever dreamed of holding it against the author as a crime and treating him as an impostor on account of it?

It is fruitless to argue that this was merely a joke, that even if the author did make this claim he had no intention of persuading anybody, that he did not in fact persuade anybody, and that the public never doubted for a moment that he himself was the author of the supposedly Greek work which he claimed to be translating. To this I should reply that a pointless joke of this kind would have been nothing but a foolish piece of childishness, that a liar is no less a liar when he fails to persuade us, and that we must distinguish between the educated public and the many simple and credulous readers who have been genuinely deceived by this manuscript story told in apparent good faith by a serious author and who have unsuspectingly drunk from what appeared to be an ancient goblet the poison of which they would at least have been wary if it had been presented to them in a modern cup.

Whether or not these distinctions are to be found in books, they are inescapable for everyone who is honest with himself and will permit himself nothing which his conscience could condemn. For it is not less of a lie to say something untrue in one's own interest than to say it to the detriment of someone else, even though the falsehood is less reprehensible. To give an advantage to someone who does not deserve it is to pervert the order of justice; falsely to attribute to oneself or to another an act which can be praised or blamed, declared innocent or guilty, is to act unjustly; and everything which by being opposed to the truth offends justice in any way is a lie. That is the line which must not be crossed, but everything which although opposed to truth does not affect justice in any way is no more than a fiction, and I confess that anyone who holds a mere fiction against himself as a lie has a more tender conscience than I have.

The lies we call white lies are real lies, because to act deceitfully in one's own interest or that of others is no less unjust than to act deceitfully against the interests of others. Whoever praises or blames untruthfully is telling a lie, if the person in question is a real person. If it is an imaginary being, he can say whatever he likes without lying, unless he makes false judgements about the morality of the facts which he has invented, since in this case, even if he is not lying about facts, he is betraying moral truth, which is infinitely superior to factual truth.

I have seen the people who are called truthful by society. Their truthfulness is confined to giving a faithful account in trivial conversations of exact times, places and names, without any embroidery or exaggeration. So long as their own interest is not involved, they are scrupulously truthful in their story-telling. But as soon as they have to talk about something that concerns them, some fact which directly involves them, they use all their eloquence to present things in the light most favourable to them, and if some lie is in their interest, even if they do not tell it themselves, they contrive to give it plausibility and have it believed without taking any responsibility for it. Such are the promptings of prudence; farewell truthfulness.

The man whom I call truthful behaves in exactly the opposite way. In matters of complete indifference, the truth which the others respect so scrupulously concerns him very little, and he will feel few qualms in amusing a gathering with invented facts which can lead to no unfair judgement either for or against any person living or dead. But any words which cause anyone to be favoured or disfavoured, admired or despised, praised or blamed against truth and justice, are a lie which will never come near his heart, his lips or his pen. He is genuinely truthful, even against his own interest, though he is little concerned to be truthful in idle conversation; he is truthful in that he seeks to deceive no one, tells the truth which injures him as faithfully as that which does him credit, and never resorts to deception either to serve his own cause or to harm his enemy. The difference between my truthful man and the others is that they are strictly faithful to any truth which costs them nothing, and that is all, whereas he is never so faithful to truth as when he has to sacrifice himself for her sake.

But, it will be said, how can one reconcile this laxity with the ardent love of truth which I have ascribed to him? Is this love a false love, since it can be adulterated in this manner? No, it is pure and unmixed; it is simply an emanation of the love of justice, and although it may often be fanciful, it strives always to avoid falsehood. For a man of this kind, justice and truth are synonyms which can be used interchangeably. The holy truth which his heart worships does not consist of trivial facts and unnecessary names, but of faithfully giving every man his due in matters which really concern him, whether it be good or evil reputation, honour or dishonour, praise or blame. He is not deceitful at the expense of others, since his sense of justice forbids this and he has no wish to harm anyone unjustly; he is not deceitful to his own advantage, because his conscience forbids this and he is incapable of appropriating what does not belong to him. Above all he is jealous of his own self-respect; this is his most valued possession and it would be a real loss to him were he to acquire the respect of others at the expense of his own. He will therefore feel no qualms in telling occasional lies about things of no importance, nor will he regard these as lies, but he will never tell lies to the advantage or disadvantage of himself or others. In all matters of historical truth, in everything concerning the behaviour of men, justice, sociability or useful knowledge, he will guard himself and his fellow-men against error as far as lies within his power. In all other matters a lie is not a lie in his eyes. If *The Temple of Gnidus* is a useful work, the story of the Greek manuscript is no more than an innocent fiction; but it is a reprehensible lie if the work is dangerous.

Such were my rules of conscience concerning truth and falsehood. My heart followed these rules automatically before they had been adopted by my reason, and my moral instinct alone showed me how to apply them. The criminal lie of which poor Marion was the victim left me with eternal remorse and this has preserved the rest of my life not only from all lies of this kind, but from all those which might in any way damage the interests and reputations of others. By imposing on myself a general prohibition of this sort I have been able to avoid having to weigh up the rights and wrongs of particular cases so as to draw a precise line between harmful lies and white lies; regarding them both as reprehensible, I have shunned them both equally.

In this as in all other matters my natural disposition has had a great influence on my principles, or rather on my habits, for I have hardly ever acted according to rules – or have hardly ever followed any other rules than the promptings of my nature. Never has a premeditated lie approached my mind, never have I lied to my own advantage; but I have often lied out of shame, to avoid embarrassment in trivial affairs or affairs that concerned only me, as when in order to keep a conversation going I have been forced by the slowness of my ideas and my lack of small talk to have recourse to fiction for something to say. When I am obliged to talk and interesting truths do not spring to mind readily enough, I invent stories rather than keep quiet, but in making up these stories I am careful as far as possible to avoid lies which would go against justice and the truth we owe to others, and to keep to fictions which are a matter of equal indifference to myself and everyone else. In doing so I should naturally prefer to put a moral truth in the place of factual truth, in other words to give a true picture of the natural affections of the human heart, and to draw some useful lesson from my stories, making them like moral tales or parables; but it would call for greater presence of mind and a readier tongue than mine to be able to make such instructive use of idle chatter. The talk runs on more quickly than my ideas and forces me to speak before thinking, so that I have often been led into foolish and inept statements which my reason had condemned and my heart disowned before I had finished speaking, but which had forestalled my judgement and thus escaped its censure.

It is also because of this irresistible instinctive reaction that when I am suddenly taken by surprise, shame and timidity often impel me to tell lies which are independent of my will but in a manner of speaking anticipate it, under the pressure of the need to give an immediate answer. The profound impression made on me by the memory of poor Marion may be capable of preventing any lies which might harm other people, but not the lies which can help me to save face when I alone am involved; yet these are just as much against my conscience and my principles as those which can have an influence on other people's lives.

I swear to Heaven that if I could instantly retract the lie which exonerates me and tell the truth which incriminates me without blackening myself still further by this recantation, I should do so with all my heart, but the shame of thus being caught in the act is a further obstacle to honesty and I feel genuine repentance without daring to make amends. An example will explain better what I mean and show that I do not lie out of personal interest or self-love, still less out of envy or malice, but simply out of embarrassment and false shame, often knowing full well that I am telling a transparent lie which can be of no use to me.

Some time ago Monsieur Foulquier persuaded me against my custom to go for a kind of alfresco dinner with him and his friend Benoit at Madame Vacassin's restaurant; our hostess and her two daughters also dined with us. During the meal the older daughter, who had recently been married and was expecting a child, suddenly looked hard at me and asked if I had had any children. Blushing all over my face, I replied that I had not had that happiness. She smiled maliciously at the company; none of this was particularly obscure even to me.

It is obvious in the first place that this was not the answer I should have given even if I had been intending to deceive them, for seeing the frame of mind of the young lady who was questioning me, I could be quite sure that no negative answer from me would change her opinion on the subject. She was expecting a negative answer, indeed she was provoking it in order to have the pleasure of making me tell a lie.[5] I was not so obtuse as not to understand that. Two minutes later the answer I should have given suddenly came to me: 'That is an indiscreet question from a young woman to a man who remained a bachelor until his old age.' By this answer, without telling a lie or having to make an embarrassing confession, I would have had the laugh on my side and taught her a little lesson which would naturally have made her somewhat less inclined to ask me impertinent questions. I did nothing of the kind, I failed to say what I should have said, I said what I should not have said – and what could not help me in the least. It is certain therefore that neither my judgement nor my will dictated my reply and that it was the automatic effect of my embarrassment. At one time I was free of embarrassment and confessed my faults with more frankness than shame, because I was sure that people would see as I did the inner qualities which redeemed them; but the eye of malice wounds and disconcerts me; I have

5. According to his own account, Rousseau's children had been placed in the Foundlings' Home in Paris.

75

grown more timid with my misfortunes, and my lies have always come from timidity.

I have never felt my natural aversion for falsehood so clearly as when I was writing my *Confessions*, for this is where I often should have been sorely tempted to lie if I had been so inclined. But far from having concealed or disguised anything which was to my disadvantage, by some strange quirk which I can hardly understand and which is perhaps due to my distaste for all forms of imitation, I felt more inclined to err on the opposite side, condemning myself too severely rather than excusing myself too indulgently, and my conscience assures me that one day I shall be judged less severely than I have judged myself. Yes, I can declare with a proud consciousness of my achievement, that in this work I carried good faith, truthfulness and frankness as far, further even, or so I believe, than any other mortal; feeling that the good outweighed the evil, it was in my interest to tell the whole truth, and that is what I did.

I never said less than the truth; sometimes I went beyond it, not in the facts but in the circumstances surrounding them, and this kind of lie was the effect of a wild imagination rather than an act of will. I am wrong to speak of lies, since none of these embellishments was really a lie. When I wrote my *Confessions* I was already old and disillusioned with the vain pleasures of life, all of which I had tasted and felt their emptiness in my heart. I was writing from memory; my memory often failed me or only provided me with an incomplete picture, and I filled the gaps with details which I dreamed up to complete my memories, but which never contradicted them. I took pleasure in dwelling on my moments of happiness and sometimes I embellished them with adornments suggested to me by my fond regrets. I described things I had forgotten as I thought they must have been, as they perhaps really had been, but never in contradiction to my actual memories. Sometimes I

martyr

decorated truth with new beauties, but I never used lies to extenuate my vices or lay false claims to virtue.

If sometimes I involuntarily concealed some blemish by presenting myself in profile, these omissions were more than made up for by other and stranger omissions, for I was often more careful to conceal my good points than my shortcomings. This is a peculiarity of my nature which men may well be forgiven for not believing, but which is no less true for being incredible. I often presented what was bad in all its baseness, but I rarely presented what was good in the most attractive light, and often I left it out altogether because it did me too much honour, and I would have seemed to be singing my own praises by writing my confessions. I described my early years without boasting of the good qualities with which I was endowed by nature – indeed I often suppressed facts which would have given them too much prominence. Let me here recall two instances from my earliest youth, both of which I remembered when writing, but rejected solely for the reason I have just given.

I used to spend nearly every Sunday at Les Pâquis at the house of a Monsieur Fazy, who had married one of my aunts and had a calico works there. One day I was in the drying room where the calender stood and I was looking at its cast-iron rollers; my eyes were tempted by their shiny appearance, I touched them with my fingers and was moving my hands up and down over the smooth cylinder with great pleasure when Monsieur Fazy's son, who had got inside the wheel, gave it a slight turn so neatly that it just caught the ends of my two longest fingers, but this was sufficient for the ends to be crushed and the two nails to be broken off. I gave a piercing yell and young Fazy cried out in alarm, got out of the wheel, threw his arms round me and begged me to be quiet, saying that it would be the end of him. At the height of my own pain I was touched by his, I stopped crying and we went to the fishpond, where he helped me to wash my hands and stop the flow of blood with moss. He beseeched me in tears not to give him away; I promised, and kept my promise so well that more than twenty years later no one knew how two of my fingers came to be scarred, for so they have remained. I was confined to my bed for more than three weeks and for over two months I was unable to use my hand, and kept repeating that a big stone had fallen on my fingers and crushed them.

> *Magnanima menzogna! or quando è il vero*
> *Sì bello che si possa a te preporre?*[6]

I was very upset by this accident however, since it happened just at the time when the citizens were due to perform their military exercises, and I and three other boys of my age had formed a group which was to take part in the exercises in uniform, together with the company of my district. I had the misery of hearing the company drum passing beneath my window with my three comrades while I lay in bed.

My other story is very similar, but comes from a later period in my life. I was playing a game of mall at Plain-Palais with one of my friends called Plince. We got into a quarrel over the game, and in the fight he gave me such a well-aimed blow of the mallet on my bare head that if he had been stronger he would have cracked my skull. I fell instantly. Never in my life have I seen anyone so distressed as that poor boy when he saw my blood flowing down my hair. He thought he had killed me. He flung himself on to me, embraced me and hugged me, weeping and uttering piercing cries. I too embraced him with all my might and shed tears in a state of confused emotion which was not entirely disagreeable. Finally he set about staunching my blood, which was still flowing, and seeing that our two handkerchiefs would not be enough, he

6. From Tasso's *Jerusalem Delivered* (II.22): 'Magnanimous falsehood! When is truth so beautiful that it can be preferred to you?'

took me off to his mother, who had a little garden close by. The good lady nearly fainted when she saw the state I was in But she managed to retain enough self-control to look after me and after washing my wound thoroughly, she treated it with lily flowers steeped in alcohol, an excellent vulnerary which is widely used in Geneva. Her tears and those of her son so affected me that for a long time afterwards I regarded her as a mother and her son as a brother, until eventually I lost sight of them both and gradually forgot them.

I said no more about this accident than the previous one, and I have had many more of the same kind which I was not even tempted to mention in my *Confessions*, so little was I seeking there to demonstrate the goodness I felt in my heart. No, when I have spoken against the truth as I knew it, it has always been about unimportant matters and has been caused more by the need to find something to say or the pleasure of writing than by my own self-interest or the advantage or disadvantage it might bring to others. And whoever reads my *Confessions* impartially – if ever this should happen – will feel that the actions I reveal are more humiliating and painful to confess than things which are more reprehensible yet less shameful, and which I have not confessed because I did not do them.

It follows from all these reflections that my professed truthfulness is based more on feelings of integrity and justice than on factual truth, and that I have been guided in practice more by the moral dictates of my conscience than by abstract notions of truth and falsehood. I have often made up stories, but very rarely told lies. In following these principles I have laid myself open to attack, but I have injured no one and I have not laid claim to more than was owing to me. In my opinion this is the only sort of truth that can be called a virtue. In all other respects it is no more than a metaphysical entity for us, and produces neither good nor evil.

Even so, I do not feel sufficiently sure in my heart of these distinctions to consider myself totally blameless. In weighing up so carefully what I owed to others, have I paid enough attention to what I owed myself? If one must act justly towards others, one must act truthfully towards oneself. Truth is an homage that the good man pays to his own dignity. When my lack of small talk forced me to fill the silence with harmless fictions, I acted wrongly, because one should not debase oneself in order to amuse others, and when the pleasure of writing led me to embellish reality with ornaments of my own invention, I acted even more wrongly, because to decorate truth with fables is in fact to disfigure it.

But what makes me most unforgivable is the motto I chose. This motto obliged me above all men to be scrupulously truthful; it was not enough always to sacrifice my interests and desires to truth, I should also have sacrificed my weakness and timidity. I should have had the courage and strength to be constantly truthful on all occasions, and never to allow fictions and fables to come from lips and a pen which were specifically dedicated to truth. This is what I should have told myself when I adopted this proud motto, and repeated to myself as long as I was bold enough to bear it. My lies were never dictated by deceitfulness, always by weakness, but this is a very poor excuse. With a weak soul one may at most be able to avoid vice, but it is arrogant and foolhardy to profess great virtues.

Such are the reflections which would probably never have entered my head were it not for Abbé Rozier's prompting. No doubt it is too late to make much use of them, but at least it is not too late to correct my judgement and regulate my will, for this is henceforth all that is in my power. In this and in all similar matters, Solon's maxim is applicable to all ages, and it is never too late to learn, even from our enemies, to be wise, truthful, modest and less presumptuous.

FIFTH WALK

OF all the places where I have lived (and I have lived in some charming ones) none has made me so truly happy or left me such tender regrets as the Island of Saint-Pierre in the middle of the Lake of Bienne. This little island, which the people of Neuchâtel call the 'Île de la Motte', is scarcely known even in Switzerland. To my knowledge it has never yet been mentioned by any traveller. Yet it is very agreeable and wonderfully well situated for the happiness of those who like to live within narrow bounds – and even if I may be the only person ever to have had such a life thrust on him by destiny, I cannot believe that I am the only one to possess so natural a taste, though I have never yet encountered it in anyone else.

The shores of the Lake of Bienne are wilder and more romantic than those of Lake Geneva, since the rocks and woods come closer to the water, but they are no less pleasing. There may be fewer ploughed fields and vineyards, fewer towns and houses, but there is more natural greenery and there are more meadows and secluded spots shaded by woodlands, more frequent and dramatic changes of scenery. Since these happy shores are free of broad roads suitable for carriages, the region is little visited by travellers, but it is fascinating for those solitary dreamers who love to drink deeply of the beauty of nature and to meditate in a silence which is unbroken but for the cry of eagles, the occasional song of birds and the roar of streams cascading down from the mountains. In the middle of this beautiful, nearly circular expanse of water lie two small islands, one of them inhabited, cultivated and some half a league in circumference, the other one smaller, uninhabited, untilled, and bound one day to be eaten away by the constant removal of earth from it to make good the damage inflicted by waves and storms upon its neighbour. Thus it is that the substance of the poor always goes to enrich the wealthy.

There is only one house in the whole island, but it is a large, pleasant and commodious one, belonging like the island to the Hospital of Bern, and inhabited by a Steward together with his family and servants. He keeps a well-stocked farmyard, with fish-ponds and runs for game-birds. Small as it is, the island is so varied in soil and situation that it contains places suitable for crops of every kind. It includes fields, vineyards, woods, orchards, and rich pastures shaded by coppices and surrounded by shrubs of every variety, all of which are kept watered by the shores of the lake; on one shore an elevated terrace planted with two rows of trees runs the length of the island, and in the middle of this terrace there is a pretty summer-house where the people who live round the lake meet and dance on Sundays during the wine harvest.

It was on this island that I took refuge after the stoning at Môtiers.[1] I found the place so delightful and so conducive to the life that suited me, that resolving to end my days there, I was concerned only lest I might not be allowed to carry out this plan, conflicting as it did with the scheme to carry me off to England, the first signs of which I was already beginning to detect. Troubled by forebodings, I could have desired that this place of refuge be made my lifelong prison, that I be shut up here for the rest of my days, deprived of any chance or hope of escaping and forbidden all communication with the mainland, so not knowing what went on in the world, I should forget its existence and be forgotten by those who lived in it.

I was barely allowed to spend two months on this island, but I could have spent two years, two centuries and all eternity

1. Rousseau's stay in the village of Môtiers near Neuchâtel had come to an end when his house was stoned one night by a group of local people, egged on by the minister Montmollin.

there without a moment's boredom, even though all the company I had, apart from Thérèse, was that of the Steward, his wife and his household – all certainly very good people, and nothing more, but this was exactly what I needed. I look upon these two months as the happiest time of my life, so happy that I would have been content to live all my life in this way, without a moment's desire for any other state.

What then was this happiness, and wherein lay this great contentment? The men of this age would never guess the answer from a description of the life I led there. Precious *far niente* was my first and greatest pleasure, and I set out to taste it in all its sweetness, and everything I did during my stay there was in fact no more than the delectable and necessary pastime of a man who has dedicated himself to idleness.

The hope that they would ask nothing better than to let me stay in the isolated place in which I had imprisoned myself, which I could not leave unaided and unobserved, and where I could have no communication or correspondence with the outside world except with the help of the people surrounding me, this hope encouraged me to hope likewise that I might end my days more peacefully than I had lived till then, and thinking that I would have all the time in the world to settle in, I began by making no attempt at all to install myself. Arriving there unexpectedly, alone and empty-handed, I sent in turn for my companion, my books and my few belongings, which I had the pleasure of leaving just as they were, unpacking not a single box or trunk and living in the house where I intended to end my days, as if it had been an inn which I was to leave the following day. Everything went along so well as it was that to try to order things better would have been to spoil them. One of my greatest joys was above all to leave my books safely shut up and to have no escritoire. When I was forced to take up my pen to answer the wretched letters I received, I reluctantly borrowed the Steward's escritoire and made haste to return it in the vain hope that I might never need to borrow it again. Instead of all these gloomy old papers and books, I filled my room with flowers and grasses, for I was then in the first flush of enthusiasm for botany, a taste soon to become a passion, which I owed to Doctor d'Ivernois. Not wanting to spend the time on serious work, I needed some agreeable pastime which would give me no more trouble than an idler likes to give himself. I set out to compose a *Flora Petrinsularis* and to describe every single plant on the island in enough detail to keep me busy for the rest of my days. They say a German once wrote a book about a lemon-skin; I could have written one about every grass in the meadows, every moss in the woods, every lichen covering the rocks – and I did not want to leave even one blade of grass or atom of vegetation without a full and detailed description. In accordance with this noble plan, every morning after breakfast, which we all took together, I would set out with a magnifying glass in my hand and my *Systema Naturae*[2] under my arm to study one particular section of the island, which I had divided for this purpose into small squares, intending to visit them all one after another in every season. Nothing could be more extraordinary than the raptures and ecstasies I felt at every discovery I made about the structure and organization of plants and the operation of the sexual parts in the process of reproduction, which was at this time completely new to me. Before progressing to rarer plants, I was delighted to observe in the common species the distinctions between families of which I had previously been completely unaware. The forking of the self-heal's two long stamens, the springiness of those of the nettle and wall pellitory, the way the seed bursts out from the fruit of the box and balsam, all these innumerable little tricks of fertilization which I was observing for the first time filled me with joy, and I went about asking people if they

2. The great work of the Swedish naturalist Linnaeus.

had seen the horns of the self-heal just as La Fontaine asked if they had read Habakkuk. After two or three hours I would come back with a rich harvest, enough to occupy me at home all the afternoon if it should rain. The rest of the morning I spent going with the Steward, his wife and Thérèse to see the labourers working at the harvest, and usually to lend them a hand; often people coming to see me from Bern found me perched up in a big tree with a bag round my waist, which I would fill with fruit and then lower to the ground on the end of a rope. My morning exercise and its attendant good humour made it very pleasant to take a rest at dinner-time, but when the meal went on too long and fine weather called me, I could not wait till the others had finished, and leaving them at table I would make my escape and install myself all alone in a boat, which I would row out into the middle of the lake when it was calm; and there, stretching out full-length in the boat and turning my eyes skyward, I let myself float and drift wherever the water took me, often for several hours on end, plunged in a host of vague yet delightful reveries, which though they had no distinct or permanent subject, were still in my eyes infinitely to be preferred to all that I had found most sweet in the so-called pleasures of life. Often reminded by the declining sun that it was time to return home, I found myself so far from the island that I was forced to row with all my might in order to arrive before nightfall. At other times, rather than strike out into the middle of the lake, I preferred to stay close to the green shores of the island, where the clear water and cool shade often tempted me to bathe. But one of my most frequent expeditions was to go from the larger island to the smaller one, disembarking and spending the afternoon there, either walking in its narrow confines among the sallows, alders, persicarias and shrubs of all kinds, or else establishing myself on the summit of a shady hillock covered with turf, wild thyme and flowers, including even red and white clover which had probably been sown there at some time in the past, a perfect home for rabbits, which could multiply there in peace, without harming anything or having anything to fear. I put the idea to the Steward, who sent for rabbits from Neuchâtel, both bucks and does, and we proceeded in great ceremony, his wife, one of his sisters, Thérèse and I, to install them on the little island, where they were beginning to breed before my departure and where they will doubtless have flourished if they have been able to withstand the rigours of winter. The founding of this little colony was a great day. The pilot of the Argonauts was not prouder than I was, when I led the company and the rabbits triumphantly from the large island to the small one; and I was gratified to see that the Steward's wife, who was extremely afraid of water and could not step into a boat without feeling unwell, embarked confidently under my command and showed no sign of fear during the crossing.

When the lake was not calm enough for boating, I would spend the afternoon roaming about the island, stopping to sit now in the most charming and isolated corners where I could dream undisturbed, and now on the terraces and little hills, where I could let my eyes wander over the beautiful and entrancing spectacle of the lake and its shores, crowned on one side by the near-by mountains and on the other extending in rich and fertile plains where the view was limited only by a more distant range of blue mountains.

As evening approached, I came down from the heights of the island, and I liked then to go and sit on the shingle in some secluded spot by the edge of the lake; there the noise of the waves and the movement of the water, taking hold of my senses and driving all other agitation from my soul, would plunge it into a delicious reverie in which night often stole upon me unawares. The ebb and flow of the water, its continuous yet undulating noise, kept lapping against my ears and

my eyes, taking the place of all the inward movements which
my reverie had calmed within me, and it was enough to
make me pleasurably aware of my existence, without troubling
myself with thought. From time to time some brief and
insubstantial reflection arose concerning the instability of the
things of this world, whose image I saw in the surface of the
water, but soon these fragile impressions gave way before the
unchanging and ceaseless movement which lulled me and without any active effort on my part occupied me so completely
that even when time and the habitual signal called me home I
could hardly bring myself to go.

After supper, when the evening was fine, we all went out
once again to walk on the terrace and breathe the coolness of
the lake air. We would sit down to rest in the summer-house,
and laugh and talk, and sing some old song which was fully
the equal of all our modern frills and fancies, and then we
would go off to bed satisfied with our day and only wishing
for the next day to be the same.

Such, apart from unforeseen and troublesome visits, was the
way I spent my time on this island during the weeks I lived
there. I should like to know what there was in it that was
attractive enough to give me such deep, tender and lasting
regrets that even fifteen years later I am incapable of thinking
of this beloved place without being overcome by pangs of
longing.

I have noticed in the changing fortunes of a long life that
the periods of the sweetest joys and keenest pleasures are not
those whose memory is most moving and attractive to me.
These brief moments of madness and passion, however
powerfully they may affect us, can because of this very power
only be infrequent points along the line of our life. They are
too rare and too short-lived to constitute a durable state, and
the happiness for which my soul longs is not made up of
fleeting moments, but of a single and lasting state, which has

no very strong impact in itself, but which by its continuance becomes so captivating that we eventually come to regard it as the height of happiness.

Everything is in constant flux on this earth. Nothing keeps the same unchanging shape, and our affections, being attached to things outside us, necessarily change and pass away as they do. Always out ahead of us or lagging behind, they recall a past which is gone or anticipate a future which may never come into being; there is nothing solid there for the heart to attach itself to. Thus our earthly joys are almost without exception the creatures of a moment; I doubt whether any of us knows the meaning of lasting happiness. Even in our keenest pleasures there is scarcely a single moment of which the heart could truthfully say: 'Would that this moment could last for ever!' And how can we give the name of happiness to a fleeting state which leaves our hearts still empty and anxious, either regretting something that is past or desiring something that is yet to come?

But if there is a state where the soul can find a resting-place secure enough to establish itself and concentrate its entire being there, with no need to remember the past or reach into the future, where time is nothing to it, where the present runs on indefinitely but this duration goes unnoticed, with no sign of the passing of time, and no other feeling of deprivation or enjoyment, pleasure or pain, desire or fear than the simple feeling of existence, a feeling that fills our soul entirely, as long as this state lasts, we can call ourselves happy, not with a poor, incomplete and relative happiness such as we find in the pleasures of life, but with a sufficient, complete and perfect happiness which leaves no emptiness to be filled in the soul. Such is the state which I often experienced on the Island of Saint-Pierre in my solitary reveries, whether I lay in a boat and drifted where the water carried me, or sat by the shores of the stormy lake, or elsewhere, on the banks of a lovely river or a stream murmuring over the stones.

What is the source of our happiness in such a state? Nothing external to us, nothing apart from ourselves and our own existence; as long as this state lasts we are self-sufficient like God. The feeling of existence unmixed with any other emotion is in itself a precious feeling of peace and contentment which would be enough to make this mode of being loved and cherished by anyone who could guard against all the earthly and sensual influences that are constantly distracting us from it in this life and troubling the joy it could give us. But most men being continually stirred by passion know little of this condition, and having only enjoyed it fleetingly and incompletely they retain no more than a dim and confused notion of it and are unaware of its true charm. Nor would it be desirable in our present state of affairs that the avid desire for these sweet ecstasies should give people a distaste for the active life which their constantly recurring needs impose upon them. But an unfortunate man who has been excluded from human society, and can do nothing more in this world to serve or benefit himself or others, may be allowed to seek in this state a compensation for human joys, a compensation which neither fortune nor mankind can take away from him.

It is true that such compensations cannot be experienced by every soul or in every situation. The heart must be at peace and its calm untroubled by any passion. The person in question must be suitably disposed and the surrounding objects conducive to his happiness. There must be neither a total calm nor too much movement, but a steady and moderate motion, with no jolts or breaks. Without any movement life is mere lethargy. If the movement is irregular or too violent it arouses us from our dreams; recalling us to an awareness of the surrounding objects, it destroys the charm of reverie and tears us from our inner self, bowing us once again beneath the yoke of fortune and mankind and reviving in us the sense of our misfortunes. Complete silence induces melancholy; it is an image of death. In such cases the assistance of a happy imagination is needed, and it comes naturally to those whom Heaven has blessed with it. The movement which does not come from outside us arises within us at such times. Our tranquillity is less complete, it is true, but it is also more agreeable when pleasant and insubstantial ideas barely touch the surface of the soul, so to speak, and do not stir its depths. One needs only enough of such ideas to allow one to be conscious of one's existence while forgetting all one's troubles. This type of reverie can be enjoyed anywhere where one is undisturbed, and I have often thought that in the Bastille, and even in a dungeon with not a single object to rest my eyes on, I could still have dreamed pleasantly.

But it must be admitted that this happened much more easily and agreeably in a fertile and lonely island, naturally circumscribed and cut off from the rest of the world, where I saw nothing but images of delight, where there was nothing to recall painful memories, where the company of the few people who lived there was attractive and pleasing without being interesting enough to absorb all my attention, and where I could devote the whole day without care or hindrance to the pastimes of my choice or to the most blissful indolence. It was without doubt a fine opportunity for a dreamer who is capable of enjoying the most delightful fantasies even in the most unpleasant settings, and who could here feed on them at leisure, enriching them with all the objects which his senses actually perceived. Emerging from a long and happy reverie, seeing myself surrounded by greenery, flowers and birds, and letting my eyes wander over the picturesque far-off shores which enclosed a vast stretch of clear and crystalline water, I fused my imaginings with these charming sights, and finding myself in the end gradually brought back to myself and my surroundings, I could not draw a line between fiction and reality; so much did everything conspire equally to make me love the contemplative and solitary life I led in that beautiful place. Would that it could come again! Would that I could go and end my days on that beloved island, never leaving it nor seeing again any inhabitants of the mainland who might recall the memory of the calamities of every kind which it has been their pleasure to heap upon me for so many years! They would soon be forgotten for ever; of course they might not similarly forget me, but what could that matter to me, so long as they were kept from troubling my quiet retreat? Set free from all the earthly passions that are born of the tumult of social life, my soul would often soar out of this atmosphere and would converse before its time with the celestial spirits whose number it hopes soon to swell. I know that mankind will never let me return to this happy sanctuary, where they did not allow me to remain. But at least they cannot prevent me from being transported there every day on the wings of imagination and tasting for several hours the same pleasures as if I were still living there. Were I there, my sweetest occupation would be to dream to my heart's content. Is it not the same thing to dream that I am there? Better still, I can add to my abstract and monotonous reveries charming images that give them life. During my moments of ecstasy the sources of these images often escaped my senses; but now, the deeper the reverie, the more vividly they are present to me. I am often more truly in their midst and they give me still greater pleasure than when I was surrounded by them. My misfortune is that as my imagination loses its fire this happens less easily and does not last so long. Alas, it is when we are beginning to leave this mortal body that it most offends us!

SIXTH WALK

THERE are very few of our automatic reactions whose cause we cannot discover in our hearts, if we are really capable of looking for it.

Yesterday, while walking along the new boulevard on my way to go botanizing on the banks of the Bièvre round Gentilly, I made a detour to the right as I was approaching the Porte d'Enfer,[1] and, cutting off through the fields, I followed the Fontainebleau road up to the heights that run parallel to this little river. This route was of no significance in itself, but recalling that I had several times automatically taken the same roundabout way, I searched myself for the cause and could not refrain from laughing when I eventually unearthed it.

In one corner of the boulevard, just by the Porte d'Enfer, a woman sets up a stall every day in summer to sell fruit, rolls and tisane. This woman has a little boy who is very sweet, but a cripple, and he hobbles about on his crutches begging from passers-by in a not unpleasant way. I had struck up a sort of acquaintance with the little fellow, and every time I went past he came up without fail to make me a little compliment, which was always followed by a little gift from me. The first few times I was delighted to see him and gave him money very willingly, and I continued doing so for some time with the same pleasure, usually even giving myself the added satisfaction of engaging him in conversation and listening to his pleasant chatter. This pleasure gradually became a habit, and thus was somehow transformed into a sort of duty which I soon began to find irksome, particularly on account of the

1. 'The new boulevard' refers to the recently opened boulevard on the Left Bank, stretching from the Invalides to the Observatory. The Porte d'Enfer was situated at the present-day Place Denfert-Rochereau.

preamble I was obliged to listen to, in which he never failed to address me as Monsieur Rousseau so as to show that he knew me well, thus making it quite clear to me on the contrary that he knew no more of me than those who had taught him. From that time on I felt less inclined to go that way, and in the end I unthinkingly adopted the habit of making a detour when I approached this obstacle.

That is what I discovered in thinking about it, for until then I had not been clearly aware of anything of the sort. This discovery then recalled successively a vast number of similar cases which proved conclusively to me that the real and basic motives of most of my actions are not as clear to me as I had long supposed. I know and feel that doing good is the truest happiness that the human heart can enjoy, but I have been denied this happiness for many years now, and so unfortunate a destiny as mine leaves little hope of performing any genuinely good deed that is both well-chosen and useful. The greatest concern of those who control my fate having been to keep me entirely surrounded by false and deceptive appearances, any occasion for virtuous behaviour is never more than a bait to tempt me into the trap they have laid for me. I know this; I know that the only good which is henceforth within my power is to abstain from acting, lest unwittingly and unintentionally I should act badly.

But there was a happier time when in following the impulses of my heart I could sometimes gladden another heart, and I owe it to my own honour to declare that whenever I could enjoy this pleasure, I found it sweeter than any other. This was a strong, pure and genuine instinct, and nothing in my heart of hearts has ever belied it. However, I often found my good deeds a burden because of the chain of duties they dragged behind them; then pleasure vanished and it became intolerably irksome to me to keep giving the same assistance which had at first delighted me. During my brief periods of prosperity, many people came to me for help, and I never refused any of them a favour that was in my power. But these first acts of charity, which I had performed with an overflowing heart, gave rise to chains of continuing obligation which I had not foreseen and which it was now impossible to shake off. My first favours were in the eyes of those who received them no more than an earnest of those that were still to come, and as soon as any unfortunate individual had me in the grip of a favour received, there was no more to be said, and that first freely chosen act of charity was transformed into an indefinite right to anything else he might subsequently need, nor was my inability to provide it enough to excuse me. In this way my dearest pleasures were transmuted into burdensome obligations.

These chains did not however seem very heavy as long as I lived obscurely and out of the general gaze. But once I had made myself public by my writings, a grave error no doubt, but one that has been more than atoned for by my misfortunes, I became the universal provider for all the needy or those who claimed to be, all the tricksters in search of a dupe, and all those who used the pretext of the great influence which they pretended to attribute to me, to attempt in one way or another to take possession of me. Then it was that I came to see that all our natural impulses, including even charity itself, can change their nature when we import them into society and follow them unthinkingly and imprudently, and can often become as harmful as they were previously useful. Many cruel experiences of this kind gradually altered my original inclinations, or rather they finally set them within their true limits and taught me to follow my tendency to good deeds less blindly when all it did was to serve the wickedness of others.

But I do not regret these experiences, since the reflections they provoked in me brought me to a new knowledge of myself and of the true motives of my behaviour on innumerable occasions when I had so often been deluded about myself. I came to see that to take pleasure in good deeds, I had to be acting freely and without constraint, and that a favour only had to become a duty for me to lose all enjoyment of it. Once this happens, the weight of obligation makes the sweetest pleasures burdensome to me, and as I said in *Émile*, I think I should have been a poor sort of husband in Turkey when a town-crier tells them it is time to perform their conjugal duties.

All this considerably alters the opinion I long had of my own virtue, for there is no virtue in following your inclinations and indulging your taste for doing good just when you feel like it; virtue consists in subordinating your inclinations to the call of duty, and of that I have been less capable than any man living. Born with a good and tender heart, compassionate to the point of weakness, and feeling my soul exalted by everything that bears the mark of magnanimity, I was led by inclination and even by passion to behave humanely, kindly and charitably as long as the appeal was only to my heart; I should have been the best and most merciful of men if I had been the most powerful, and to rid me of any desire for vengeance it would have been enough for me to be in a position to avenge myself. I should even have had no difficulty in acting justly against my own interests, but I should never have been able to bring myself to do this against the interests of those who were dear to me. As soon as my duty came into conflict with the promptings of my heart, the victory rarely went to the former, unless I only had to abstain from action; on such occasions I generally conquered my inclinations, but I always found it impossible to take any positive action against my natural leanings. Whether the command comes from other people, duty or even necessity, when my heart is silent, my will remains deaf and I cannot obey. I see the evil which threatens me and I let it happen rather than exerting myself to prevent it. Often I begin by making an effort, but very soon this effort tires and exhausts me; I cannot persevere. In every imaginable field of activity, I soon find it impossible to do anything that I cannot do with pleasure.

This is not all. When obligation concurs with my own desires, this is enough to quench them and transform them into reluctance or even aversion, if the obligation is too pressing; this is what makes good deeds irksome when they are demanded of me, even though I did them of my own accord when they were not demanded of me. A purely voluntary good deed is certainly something that I like doing. But when the recipient uses it as a claim on further favours and rewards me with hate if I refuse, when he insists on my being his perpetual benefactor just because I initially took pleasure in helping him, then charity becomes burdensome and pleasure vanishes. If I give in, it is out of weakness and false shame, but my heart is not in it, and far from feeling pleased with myself, I reproach myself inwardly for doing good against my will.

I know that there is a kind of contract, indeed the most sacred of contracts, between the benefactor and the recipient; together they form a kind of society, which is more closely knit than the society which unites men in general, and if the recipient tacitly promises his gratitude, the benefactor likewise commits himself to continue showing the same kindness as long as the recipient remains worthy of it, and to repeat his acts of charity whenever he is asked and is capable of doing so. These are not explicit conditions, but they are the natural consequences of the relationship which has just come into being. A person who refuses a gratuitous favour the first time it is asked of him gives the person he refuses no grounds for complaint, but anyone who in a similar situation refuses the same person the same favour which he had previously granted, frustrates a hope which his behaviour has authorized; he disappoints and belies an expectation which he himself has brought into being. This refusal is felt as being harsher and more unjust than the former, but nevertheless it is the product of an independence which is dear to our hearts and cannot be relinquished without difficulty. When I pay a debt, I am performing a duty; when I make a gift, I am indulging in a pleasure. But the pleasure of doing our duty is one which only the habit of virtue can produce in us; those pleasures which come to us directly from nature are less exalted.

After so many unhappy experiences I have learned to foresee the consequences of following my immediate inclinations, and I have often abstained from a good deed which I was able and anxious to do, fearing the enslavement which I would bring upon myself if I gave way to it unthinkingly. I did not always have such fears; on the contrary, in my youth my affection for others grew by my own acts of kindness, and similarly I have often found that those whom I helped became attached to me more from gratitude than self-interest. But things changed utterly in this respect as in all the rest, as soon as my misfortunes began. Since then I have lived among a different generation quite unlike the first, and my own feelings for others have suffered from the changes I have observed in theirs. The same people whom I have seen successively in these very different generations, have as it were adapted themselves successively first to the one and then to the other. Formerly frank and truthful, they have followed the general example in becoming what they now are, and the mere fact that the times have changed has meant that people have changed accordingly. How could I preserve the same feelings for them, when they display qualities opposed to those that first produced these feelings? I do not hate them, because I cannot hate, but I cannot repress the scorn which they deserve, nor prevent myself from letting them see it.

Perhaps I too, without noticing it, have changed more than I should have done. What sort of character could withstand a situation like mine without deteriorating? Convinced by twenty years' experience that all the good inclinations which my heart received from the hands of nature have been twisted by my fate and those who control it to my own disadvantage or that of others, I can now only regard a good deed which is suggested to me as a trap to lure me into something bad. I know that whatever the result of my action, my good intention will still be equally commendable. This is doubtless true, but the inner charm will be lacking, and if that is not there to spur me on, I feel nothing but cold indifference in my heart; and in the certainty that instead of being genuinely useful, I shall merely be acting the dupe, wounded in my self-love and dissuaded by my reason, I feel only reluctance and unwillingness where naturally I should have been burning with eagerness to help.

There are types of adversity which elevate and strengthen the soul, but there are others which depress and crush it; such is the one of which I am a victim. If there had been the slightest leaven of evil in my soul, this adversity would have fermented it to excess and driven me into a frenzy, but it only succeeded in reducing me to inactivity. Unable to do good to myself or anyone else, I abstain from acting; and this state, which is only blameless because I cannot avoid it, makes me find a sort of satisfaction in abandoning myself completely and without reproach to my natural inclination. No doubt I go too far, since I avoid opportunities for action even when I think nothing but good can come of them. But knowing that I am not allowed to see things as they are, I refrain from judging by the appearances my enemies give to things, and however alluring the motives for action may seem, it is enough that they have been left within my grasp for me to be sure they are deceptive.

I was still a child when fate apparently laid the first trap, which for a long time made me so prone to fall into all the rest. I was born the most trusting of men, and for forty whole years this trust was never once betrayed. Suddenly plunged into a new order of things, surrounded by a new kind of people, I stumbled into a thousand snares without noticing a single one of them, and twenty years' experience has hardly been enough to open my eyes to my destiny. Once I had been convinced that there is nothing but falsehood and deceit in the extravagant protestations of friendship that are showered on me, I quickly went to the opposite extreme, for once we have taken leave of our true nature, there are no limits to what we may become. From then on I grew sick of men, and my own desires, which concur with theirs in this respect, keep me further removed from them than all their stratagems.

Try as they may, they will never transform this distaste into total aversion. When I think of the way they have made themselves dependent on me in their attempt to make me dependent on them, I feel genuinely sorry for them. If I am not unhappy, this makes them unhappy, and every time I consider my situation, I find that they are the unfortunate ones. Perhaps pride has a part in these judgements. I feel too much above them to hate them. They may provoke my scorn, but never my hatred; indeed I love myself too much to be able to hate any man. To do so would be to limit and confine my existence, whereas I would prefer to expand it to include the whole universe.

I would rather flee from them than hate them. The sight of them affects my senses and thence my heart with impressions which are made painful by all their cruel looks, but my distress ceases as soon as its cause disappears. Their presence affects me in spite of myself, but never the memory of them. When I do not see them, it is as if they did not exist for me.

Even my indifference towards them only concerns their

relations with me, for in their relations with one another, they still arouse my sympathy, and I can feel for them as I would for characters in a play. My moral being would have to be annihilated for me to lose interest in justice. The sight of injustice and wickedness still makes my blood boil with anger; virtuous actions where I see no trace of ostentation or vain-glory always make me tremble with joy, and even now they fill my eyes with tears of happiness. But I must see and judge them for myself, for after what has happened to me I should have to be mad to adopt the judgement of men on any matter or to take anyone's word for anything.

If my face and features were as completely unknown to men as my character and natural disposition, I should be able to live among them without suffering, indeed I might take pleasure in their company as long as I was a complete stranger to them; abandoning myself freely to my natural inclinations, I should still love them if they paid no attention to me. I should display a universal and totally disinterested benevolence towards them, but without ever attaching myself to anyone in particular or submitting to the yoke of any obligations, and in all things I should behave towards them freely and of my own accord as they have so much difficulty in behaving, spurred on as they are by their self-love and hampered by all their laws.

If I had remained free, unknown and isolated, as nature meant me to be, I should have done nothing but good, for my heart does not contain the seeds of any harmful passion. If I had been invisible and powerful like God, I should have been good and beneficent like him. It is strength and freedom which make really good men; weakness and slavery have never produced anything but evil-doers. If I had possessed the ring of Gyges,[2] it would have made me independent of men and

2. According to legend King Gyges of Lydia killed his predecessor thanks to a ring which made him invisible.

made them dependent on me. I have often wondered, in my castles in the air, how I should have used this ring, for in such a case power must indeed be closely followed by the temptation to abuse it. Able to satisfy my desires, capable of doing anything without being deceived by anyone, what might I have desired at all consistently? One thing only: to see every heart contented; the sight of general happiness is the only thing that could have given me lasting satisfaction, and the ardent desire to contribute to it would have been my most constant passion. Always impartially just and unfalteringly good, I should have guarded myself equally against blind mistrust and implacable hate, because seeing men as they are and reading their inmost thoughts without difficulty, I should have found few who were likeable enough to deserve my full affection and few who were odious enough to deserve my hate, and also because their very wickedness would have inclined me to pity them out of the sure knowledge of the harm they do themselves in seeking to harm others. Perhaps in my light-hearted moments I should have had the childish impulse to work the occasional miracle, but being entirely disinterested and obeying only my natural inclinations, I should have performed scores of merciful or equitable ones for every act of just severity. As the minister of Providence, meting out its laws according to my power, I should have worked more sensible and useful miracles than those of the Golden Legend or the tomb of Saint Medard.[3]

There is only one point on which the ability to go everywhere unobserved might have presented me with temptations that I should have found it hard to resist, and once I had strayed into these ways of perdition, where might they not have led me? It would be showing great ignorance of human nature

3. This refers to the supposed miracles worked on the tomb of the Jansenist Deacon Pâris in the cemetery of St Medard between 1727 and 1732.

and of myself to flatter myself that such an opportunity would not have led me astray or that reason would have halted me on this downward path. I could be sure of myself in every other respect, but this would be my ruin. The man whose power sets him above humanity must himself be above all human weaknesses, or this excess of power will only serve to sink him lower than his fellows, and lower than he would himself have been had he remained their equal.

All things considered, I think it best to throw away my magic ring before it makes me do something foolish. If men insist on seeing me as other than I am and are provoked into injustice by the mere sight of me, in order to spare them this sight it is better to flee their presence than remain invisible in their midst. It is up to them to conceal their actions from me, disguising their stratagems, avoiding the light of day, burrowing like moles deep into the earth. As for me, let them see me if they can, so much the better; but this is beyond them, instead of me they will never see anyone but the Jean-Jacques they have created and fashioned for themselves so that they can hate me to their heart's content. I should be wrong then to be upset by the image they have of me; I ought to take no real interest in it, since it is not me that they are seeing.

The conclusion I can draw from all these reflections is that I have never been truly fitted for social life, where there is nothing but irksome duty and obligation, and that my independent character has always made it impossible for me to submit to the constraints which must be accepted by anyone who wishes to live among men. As long as I act freely I am good and do nothing but good, but as soon as I feel the yoke of necessity or human society I become rebellious, or rather recalcitrant, and then I am of no account. When I ought to do the opposite of what I want, nothing will make me do it, but neither do I do what I want, because I am too weak. I abstain from acting, because my weakness is all in the domain of action, my strength is all negative, and my sins are all sins of omission, rarely sins of commission. I have never believed that man's freedom consists in doing what he wants, but rather in never doing what he does not want to do, and this is the freedom I have always sought after and often achieved, the freedom by virtue of which I have most scandalized my contemporaries. For they, being active, busy, ambitious, detesting freedom in others and not desiring it for themselves, as long as they can sometimes have their way, or rather prevent others from having theirs, they force themselves all their lives to do what they do not want to do and are willing to endure any servitude in order to command. They were wrong then, not in expelling me as a useless member of society, but in ostracizing me as dangerous, for I confess that I have done very little good, but never in my life have I harboured evil intentions, and I doubt if there is any man living who has done less actual evil than I.

SEVENTH WALK

I HAVE only just begun to write down all my long reveries and already I can feel that I shall soon have finished. Another pastime has taken over and now absorbs me so completely that I have not even time for dreaming. I abandon myself to it with an enthusiasm bordering on extravagance, and which makes me laugh when I think about it, yet I continue undeterred, because in my present situation I have no other rule of conduct than always to follow freely my natural leanings. I can do nothing to change my fate, all my inclinations are innocent, and since all the judgements of men are henceforward as nothing to me, wisdom itself suggests that both in public and in private I should do all I want that remains within my power, with no guide but my own desires and no restraint but the weakness that comes with age. So I am left with my grasses to keep me going and botany to occupy my mind. I was already an old man when I got my first smattering of it in Switzerland from Doctor d'Ivernois, and during my travels I botanized successfully enough to gain a fair knowledge of the vegetable kingdom. But in my sixties, living a sedentary life in Paris, beginning to lose the strength required for long botanical expeditions, and in any case sufficiently occupied with music-copying not to need any other activity, I had given up a pastime which was no longer necessary to me; I had sold my herbarium and sold my books, contenting myself with occasionally identifying the common plants which I found on my walks round Paris; during this time the little I knew vanished almost completely from my memory, far more quickly than it was imprinted on it.

Suddenly, with my sixty-fifth birthday already behind me, having lost both the little memory I had and such strength as remained to me for roaming the countryside, with no guide, no books, no garden, no herbarium, here I am once again possessed by this madness, and even more violently than when it first took hold of me; here I am seriously considering the wise plan of learning all of Murray's[1] *Regnum Vegetabile* and acquainting myself with every known plant. Not having the means to buy the botany textbooks once again, I have set myself to copy out those that have been lent me, and having resolved to reconstitute a herbarium more complete than my previous one, until such time as I can collect all the plants of the seashore and the Alps, and the flowers of all the trees of the Indies, I am making a modest beginning with chickweed, chervil, borage and groundsel. I botanize learnedly at my bird-cage, and every new blade of grass that I spot makes me say to myself with satisfaction: 'There's one more plant anyhow.'

I am not trying to defend my decision to follow this whim; it seems very reasonable to me, persuaded as I am that in my present situation to devote myself to the pastimes that appeal to me is not only very wise, but very virtuous into the bargain: it is a way of preventing any seeds of vengeance or hate from taking root in my heart, and in my position to be able to take pleasure in any pastime is a sure sign of a character totally free of all the irascible passions. It is my way of taking my revenge on my persecutors; I could not find any more cruel punishment for them than to be happy in spite of them.

Yes, there can be no doubt that reason allows and even directs me to give way to any inclination that attracts me when nothing prevents me from following it, but it does not tell me why this particular activity should attract me and what charm I can find in a fruitless study where I neither make any progress nor learn anything useful, a study which takes an old dotard like me, feeble, ponderous, slow-witted and absent-minded as

1. Joannes Andreas Murray, a Swedish disciple of Linnaeus.

I am, back to school-room exercises and childhood lessons. It is a strange choice and I should like to know the explanation for it. I think that, properly understood, it might add something new to the self-knowledge which I have devoted my last hours of leisure to acquiring.

Sometimes I have thought quite profoundly, but this has rarely given me any pleasure and has almost always been done against my will and under duress as it were; reverie amuses and distracts me, thought wearies and depresses me; thinking has always been for me a disagreeable and thankless occupation. Sometimes my reveries end in meditation, but more often my meditations end in reverie, and during these wanderings my soul roams and soars through the universe on the wings of imagination, in ecstasies which surpass all other pleasures.

For as long as I enjoyed this in all its purity, all other occupations were always uninteresting to me. But when, thrown by outside forces into a literary career, I came to know the weariness of mental labour and the cares of inauspicious fame, I also felt my sweet reveries languish and fade away, and before long, being forced against my will to concern myself with my sad fate, I could only rarely recapture those sweet ecstasies which for fifty years had taken the place of fame and fortune and, demanding no other expenditure than that of time, had made me in my idleness the happiest of mortals.

It was even to be feared that my imagination, alarmed by my misfortunes, might end by filling my reveries with them, and the continual consciousness of my sufferings might gradually come to oppress my heart and crush me finally under their weight. In these circumstances an instinct that is natural to me averted my eyes from every depressing thought, silenced my imagination and, fixing my attention on the objects surrounding me, made me look closely for the first time at the details of the great pageant of nature, which until then I had hardly ever contemplated otherwise than as a total and undivided spectacle.

Trees, bushes and plants are the clothing and adornment of the earth. There is no sight so sad as a bare, barren countryside that presents the eyes with nothing but stones, mud and sand. But brought to life by nature and dressed in her wedding dress amidst the running waters and the song of birds, earth in the harmony of her three kingdoms offers man a living, fascinating and enchanting spectacle, the only one of which his eyes and his heart can never grow weary.

The more sensitive the soul of the observer, the greater the ecstasy aroused in him by this harmony. At such times his senses are possessed by a deep and delightful reverie, and in a state of blissful self-abandonment he loses himself in the immensity of this beautiful order, with which he feels himself at one. All individual objects escape him; he sees and feels nothing but the unity of all things. His ideas have to be restricted and his imagination limited by some particular circumstances for him to observe the separate parts of this universe which he was striving to embrace in its entirety.

This is what occurred naturally in me when my heart was constricted by misery and gathered all its impulses tightly around itself so as to preserve its last remnants of warmth, which were on the point of vanishing altogether in my growing depression. I wandered aimlessly in the woods and mountains, not daring to think for fear of increasing my unhappiness. My imagination, which shuns all painful objects, allowed my senses to yield to the slight but pleasant impressions of my surroundings. My eyes strayed unceasingly from one thing to another and inevitably among so great a variety of objects there were some which attracted my attention and held it for longer.

I came to enjoy this recreation of the eyes, which relaxes and amuses the mind, taking it off our misfortunes and making us forget our sufferings. The nature of the objects contributes greatly to this distraction and adds to its charm. Sweet smells, bright colours and the most elegant shapes seem to vie for our attention. One has only to love pleasure in order to yield to such delightful sensations, and if everyone is not equally affected by these impressions, it is because some are lacking in natural sensibility and the majority are so preoccupied by other ideas that their mind only lends itself surreptitiously to the objects which strike their senses.

There is one further thing that helps to deter people of taste from taking an interest in the vegetable kingdom. This is the habit of considering plants only as a source of drugs and medicines. The philosopher Theophrastus approached them quite differently, and can be thought of as the sole botanist of antiquity; as a result he is virtually unknown among us. But thanks to a certain Dioscorides, a great compiler of nostrums, and to his commentators, medicine has so seized on the plants and transformed them into medicaments that we hardly see anything in them except something that does not really exist, the supposed curative virtues ascribed to them by every Tom, Dick or Harry. No one imagines that the structure of plants could deserve any attention in its own right; people who spend their lives on the learned classification of shells look down on botany as a useless study unless it includes what they call the study of properties, that is to say, unless one abandons the observation of nature, which does not lie and which tells us nothing of such things, and submits solely to the authority of men, who are liars and assert a great many things for which we have to take their word – and this in its turn is usually based on the authority of others. Linger in some meadow studying one by one all the flowers that adorn it, and people will take you for a herbalist and ask you for something to cure the itch in children, scab in men, or glanders in horses.

This distasteful prejudice has been partially removed in other countries, especially England, thanks to Linnaeus, who has gone some way towards rescuing botany from the schools of pharmacy and restoring it to natural history and agronomy, but in France, where this science has found little favour among people of fashion, they have remained so barbarous in this respect that a Paris wit who saw a collector's garden in London full of rare plants and trees, could only exclaim by way of praise: 'What a splendid garden for an apothecary!' In that case Adam was the first apothecary, for it is hard to imagine a garden with a better collection of plants than the Garden of Eden.

These medicinal associations are certainly ill suited to make botany an attractive study; they tarnish the colour of the meadows and the brilliance of the flowers, they drain the woods of all freshness and make the green leaves and the shade seem dull and disagreeable. All the charming and gracious details of the structure of plants hold little interest for anyone whose sole aim is to pound them all up in a mortar, and it is no good seeking garlands for shepherdesses among the ingredients of an enema.

My country thoughts were unsullied by all this pharmacology; nothing was further from my mind than infusions and poultices. I have often reflected, as I studied the fields, the orchards, the woods and all the plants that live in them, that the vegetable kingdom is a plentiful store of food given by nature to man and the animals. But never did it occur to me to look there for drugs and medicines. In all the many productions of nature I see nothing that could prompt us to use them in this way, and nature would have given us some sign if she had ordained some particular plants for our use, as she has for the things we eat. Indeed I feel that the pleasure I take in roaming the woodlands would be soured by the idea of human ailments, if this made me think of fevers, stones, gout and epilepsy. However, I shall not deny to plants the great powers attributed to them; I shall merely say that if they do indeed possess these powers, it is out of sheer malice that our invalids fail to recover, for of all the illnesses that men give themselves there is not one that cannot be totally cured by twenty different herbs.

This attitude which always brings everything back to our material interest, causing us to seek in all things either profits or remedies, and which if we were always in good health would leave us indifferent to all the works of nature, has never been an attitude of mine. In this I am diametrically opposed to other men: everything that concerns my needs saddens and sours my thoughts, and I never found any real charm in the pleasures of the mind unless I was able to forget all about the interests of my body. Thus even if I believed in medicine, even if I found its remedies attractive, they could never bring me the joy that comes from pure and disinterested contemplation, and my soul could never take wings and soar above the natural world as long as I felt it to be tied to the needs of the body. Moreover, though I never had much belief in medicine, I had a great deal in certain doctors whom I liked and held in high esteem, giving them complete authority over my carcass. Fifteen years of experience have made me wiser to my cost; now I let myself be ruled once again by the laws of nature alone, and she has restored me to my original health. Even if the doctors had no other grievance against me, who could be surprised that they hate me? I am the living proof of the vanity of their art and the uselessness of their remedies.

No, nothing that is personal, nothing that involves the interests of my body, can truly possess my soul. My meditations and reveries are never more delightful than when I can forget myself. I feel transports of joy and inexpressible raptures in becoming fused as it were with the great system of beings and identifying myself with the whole of nature. As long as all men were my brothers, I invented plans of earthly happiness for myself; these plans were always universal in scope, I could be happy only in the happiness of all and my heart was never touched by the idea of private happiness, until I saw my brothers seek their own happiness in my misery. In order not to hate them I had no other choice but to flee from them, and taking refuge in the bosom of our common mother, I tried in her embrace to avoid the attacks of her children, I became a solitary or, as they say, an unsociable misanthropist, because I prefer the harshest solitude to the society of malicious men which thrives only on treachery and hate.

Forced to refrain from thinking for fear of thinking in spite of myself about my misfortunes, forced to repress what remained of a happy yet flagging imagination, which might eventually have been alarmed by so much affliction, forced to try and forget humanity and all the ignominy and outrages they shower upon me, lest indignation should finally make me bitter against them, even so I cannot concentrate my thoughts entirely within myself, because independently of my will my expansive soul seeks to extend its feelings and its existence to other beings, and I cannot as I once did throw myself head-long into this great ocean of nature, because my enfeebled and diminished faculties can no longer find any objects sufficiently distinct, stable and accessible to give them a firm hold, and I no longer feel vigorous enough to swim in the chaos of my former ecstasies. My ideas are hardly more than sensations now, and my understanding cannot transcend the objects which form my immediate surroundings.

Fleeing from men, seeking solitude, no longer using my imagination and thinking even less, yet endowed with a lively nature that keeps me from languid and melancholy apathy, I began to take an interest in everything around me, and a quite natural instinct led me to prefer those objects which were most pleasing to me. The mineral kingdom possesses no intrinsic charm or attraction: buried deep in the bosom of the earth its riches seem to have been placed far from the eyes of men so as not to arouse their cupidity. They are there as a kind of reserve, destined in due course to be added to those true riches which lie more easily within man's reach and for which he gradually loses the taste as he grows more corrupt. Then he has to call on ingenuity, drudgery and toil to assist him in his need; he scours the entrails of the earth and descends into its depths, risking his life and health, in search of imaginary gains to replace the true blessings which it offered him spontaneously when he was capable of enjoying them. He flees the sun and the light, which he is no longer worthy of seeing, he buries himself alive, and rightly so, since he no longer deserves to live in the light of day. Then quarries, pits, forges, furnaces and a world of anvils, hammers, smoke and flame take the place of the sweet images of rustic labour. Haggard faces of wretches languishing in the foul vapours of the pits, black Vulcans and hideous Cyclops, this is the picture that the mines offer us deep down in the earth, in place of the sight of verdure and flowers, azure sky, loving shepherds and sturdy labourers on its surface.

It is easy, I admit, to go around picking up sand and stones, filling your pockets and your study with them and thus giving yourself the appearance of a naturalist; but those who are content to make collections of this kind are usually rich and ignorant people who only want the pleasure of showing off their science. In order to profit from the study of minerals one has to be a chemist or a physicist, perfoming laborious and costly experiments, working in laboratories, spending a great deal of money and time surrounded by coal, crucibles, furnaces, retorts, smoke and suffocating fumes, constantly risking one's life and often damaging one's health. All this miserable and wearisome work usually produces more vanity than knowledge: show me even the most mediocre chemist who does not believe that he has fathomed all the great works of nature just because he has chanced to come across some little tricks of art.

The animal kingdom is more within our reach and certainly more deserving of study. But after all, are there not difficulties, obstacles, troubles and vexations attached to this pursuit also, particularly for a solitary who can expect no help from anybody in his amusements or his labours? How is one to observe, dissect, study and become familiar with the birds in the air, the fish in the water, or the quadrupeds, which are swifter than the wind and stronger than man, and are no more inclined to come and be studied than I am to run after them and subject them by force to my investigations? I should have then to fall back on snails, worms and flies, and my life would be spent chasing butterflies till I was out of breath, impaling poor insects, dissecting such mice as I could catch or else the carcasses of animals I happened to find dead. The study of animals is worthless without anatomy, which teaches us how to classify them and distinguish the families and species. In order to study their behaviour and natural characteristics I should need aviaries, fish-pools and cages; I should somehow have to force them to stay within reach; I have neither the desire nor the means to keep them in captivity nor have I the necessary agility to run after them when they are free. So I should have to study them dead, to tear them apart, remove their bones, dig deep into their palpitating entrails! What a terrible sight an anatomy theatre is! Stinking corpses, livid running flesh, blood, repellent intestines, horrible skeletons, pestilential vapours! Believe me, that is not the place where Jean-Jacques will go looking for amusement.

Bright flowers, adornment of the meadows, cool shades, streams, woods and green glades, come and purify my imagination of all these hideous images. My soul, being dead to all sublime impulses, can no longer be touched by anything except through the senses; only sensation is left me, and it alone can now bring me pleasure or pain in this world. Attracted by the charming objects that surround me, I look at them, observe them carefully, compare them, and eventually learn to classify them, and lo and behold, I am as much of a botanist as anyone needs to be who only wants to study nature in order to discover ever new reasons for loving her.

I do not seek to educate myself; it is too late for that. In any case, I have never known all this science to contribute to our happiness in life; my aim is to find a simple and pleasant pastime which I can enjoy without effort and which will distract me from my misfortunes. It costs me neither money nor care to roam nonchalantly from plant to plant and flower to flower, examining them, comparing their different characteristics, noting their similarities and differences, and finally studying the organization of plants so as to be able to follow the intricate working of these living mechanisms, to succeed occasionally in discovering their general laws and the reason and purpose of their varied structures, and to give myself up to the pleasure of grateful admiration of the hand that allows me to enjoy all this.

Plants seem to have been scattered profusely over the face of the earth like the stars in heaven, so that the lure of pleasure and curiosity should lead men to study nature. But the stars are far above us; we need preliminary instruction, instruments and machines, which are like so many immense ladders enabling us to approach them and bring them within our grasp. Plants have been placed within our reach by nature herself; they spring up beneath our feet, in our hands so to speak, and even if their essential parts are sometimes so small as to be invisible to the naked eye, the instruments which bring them nearer to us are far simpler to use than those of the astronomer. Botany is the ideal study for the idle, unoccupied solitary; a blade and a magnifying glass are all the equipment he needs for his observations. He wanders about, passing freely from one object to another, he considers each plant in turn with interest and curiosity, and as soon as he begins to grasp the laws of their structure he receives from his observations an effortless pleasure as intense as if it had cost him a great deal of labour. This ideal occupation has a charm which can only be felt when the passions are entirely at rest, but which is then enough to make our lives pleasant and happy; but as soon as our self-interest or vanity are brought into play and we are concerned to obtain positions or write books, as soon as we learn only in order to teach, and devote ourselves to botany merely for the sake of becoming authors or professors, all this sweet charm vanishes, we see plants simply as the instruments of our passions, we take no real pleasure in studying them, we do not want to know, but to show that we know, and the woods become for us merely a public stage where we seek applause – or else, confining our attention to the study or at best the botanical garden, rather than observing plants in their natural setting, we concern ourselves solely with systems and methods, a subject for endless argument, but which does not discover a single unknown plant or throw any real light on natural history or the vegetable kingdom. Thence come all the hate and jealousy that the struggle for fame arouses in authors of botanical works just as much as in other scholars – perhaps even more so. They distort this delightful study, robbing it of its true nature and transplanting it to towns and academies, where it degenerates no less than exotic plants in the gardens of collectors.

A quite different attitude of mind has made this study a kind of passion to me, a passion that fills the gap left by all those I no longer feel. I scale rocks and mountains, or bury myself in valleys and woods, so as to hide as far as I can from the memory of men and the attacks of the wicked. Deep in the forest shades it seems to me that I can live free, forgotten and undisturbed as if I no longer had any enemies, or as if the foliage of the woods could protect me from their attacks as it obliterates them from my mind, and in my folly I imagine that if I do not think of them, they will not think of me. This illusion gives me such satisfaction that I would abandon myself to it completely, if my position, my weakness and my needs allowed me to do so. The deeper the solitude that surrounds me, the greater the need I feel at such times for something to fill this vacuum, and where my imagination cannot provide me with ideas or my memory rejects them, the earth makes up for this with the many objects which it produces spontaneously, without any human agency, and sets before my eyes on all sides. The pleasure of going to some lonely spot in search of new plants is combined with that of escaping from my persecutors, and when I reach places where there is no trace of men I breathe freely, as if I were in a refuge where their hate could no longer pursue me.

I shall remember all my life a botanical expedition I once made on the slopes of the Robeila, a mountain belonging to Justice Clerc.[2] I was alone, I made my way far into the crevices of the rocks, and going from thicket to thicket and rock to rock I finally reached a corner so deeply hidden away that I do not think I have ever seen a wilder spot. Black fir trees were mingled and intertwined with gigantic beeches, several of which had fallen with age, and they formed an impenetrable barrier round this secret refuge; through the few gaps in this dark wall one could see nothing but sheer rock faces and fearful precipices which I dared only look at lying flat on my face. From the mountain gorges came the cry of the horned owl, the little owl and the eagle, while from time to time some more familiar birds lightened the horror of this solitary place. Here I found seven-leaved coral-wort, cyclamen,

2. In the region of Môtiers, where Rousseau had lived from 1763 to 1765.

nidus avis, the large *laserpitium* and a few other plants which occupied and delighted me for a long time, but gradually succumbing to the powerful impression of my surroundings, I forgot about botany and plants, sat down on pillows of *lycopodium* and mosses, and began dreaming to my heart's content, imagining that I was in a sanctuary unknown to the whole universe, a place where my persecutors would never find me out. Soon this reverie became tinged with a feeling of pride. I compared myself to those great explorers who discover a desert island, and said complacently to myself: 'Doubtless I am the first mortal to set foot in this place.' I considered myself well-nigh a second Columbus. While I was preening myself on this notion, I heard not far off a certain clicking noise which sounded familiar. I listened: the same noise came again, then it was repeated many times over. Surprised and intrigued, I got up, pushed through a thicket of undergrowth in the direction of the noise, and in a hollow twenty yards from the very place where I had thought to be the first person to tread, I saw a stocking mill.

I cannot express the confused and contradictory emotions which this discovery stirred up in me. My first reaction was one of joy at finding myself among human beings where I had thought I was quite alone, but this reaction, which came like a flash of lightning, quickly gave way to a more lasting feeling of distress at not being able, even in the depths of the Alps, to escape from the cruel hands of men intent on persecuting me. For I could be certain that there were scarcely two men in this mill who were not a party to the plot which was organized by the minister Montmollin,[3] but which had its causes further back. I quickly banished this gloomy thought from my mind and finished by laughing at myself, both at my childish vanity and at the comic punishment it had received.

3. See note on p. 82.

But after all, who could have anticipated finding a factory surrounded by precipices? Switzerland is the one country in the world where you can find this mixture of wild nature and human industry. The whole of Switzerland is like one great city, whose long wide streets, longer than the Rue Saint-Antoine, are planted with forests and broken up by mountains, and whose scattered and isolated houses are only connected with one another by English landscape gardens. In this connection I recalled another botanical expedition, which Du Peyrou d'Escherny, Colonel Pury, Justice Clerc and I had undertaken some time before on the Chasseron mountain, from whose summit one can see seven lakes. We were told that there was only one house on this mountain, and we should never have guessed the profession of its occupant if they had not added that he was a bookseller, and what is more, that he did a thriving trade in the region. I think a single fact of this sort gives a better idea of Switzerland than all the accounts given by travellers.

Here is another story of more or less the same kind, which gives an equally good idea of a very different people. During my stay in Grenoble I often went on short botanical outings near the town with a local lawyer, Monsieur Bovier, not that he knew or cared about botany, but he had appointed himself my watchdog and made it a rule as far as possible never to let me out of his sight. One day we were walking by the Isère in a place full of buckthorns. I saw some ripe berries on these bushes, tried one or two out of curiosity, and finding that they had a very pleasant, mildly acid taste, I began eating them to quench my thirst; the worthy Monsieur Bovier stood by and watched me without either imitating me or saying a single word. One of his friends came by and seeing me nibbling these berries, said to me: 'Whatever are you doing, Monsieur? Don't you know those fruit are poisonous?' 'Poisonous!' I exclaimed in surprise. 'Of course,' he answered, 'and every one knows it; no one from here ever dreams of eating them.' I looked at Monsieur Bovier and asked him: 'Why didn't you warn me then?' 'Oh, Monsieur,' he replied respectfully, 'I didn't dare to take the liberty.' I burst out laughing at this example of Dauphiné humility, but even so I put an end to my little meal. I was convinced, as I still am, that no natural product which has a pleasant taste can be harmful to us unless we take excessive quantities of it. However, I must admit that I kept a watch on myself for the rest of that day, but I escaped with nothing more than a little anxiety; I ate supper with an excellent appetite, slept better still, and got up the next morning in perfect health after swallowing the previous day fifteen or twenty berries of this terrible *hippophae*, which is poisonous even in very small doses according to what I was told in Grenoble the next day. This little adventure so amused me that I never remember it without laughing at Lawyer Bovier's singular discretion.

All my botanical walks, the varied impressions made by the places where I have seen memorable things, the ideas they have aroused in me, all this has left me with impressions which are revived by the sight of the plants I have collected in those places. I shall never again see those beautiful landscapes, those forests, those lakes, those groves, those rocks or those mountains, the sight of which has always moved me, but now that I can no longer roam in those happy places, I have only to open my flower collection to be transported there. The fragments of plant life which I picked there are enough to bring back the whole magnificent spectacle. This collection is like a diary of my expeditions, which makes me set out again with renewed joy, or like an optical device which places them once again before my eyes.

It is the chain of accessory ideas that makes me love botany. It brings together and recalls to my imagination all the images which most charm it: meadows, waters, woods, solitude and above all the peace and tranquillity which one can find in these places – all of this it instantly conjures up before my memory. It makes me forget the persecutions of men, their hate, their scorn, their insults and all the evil deeds with which they have repaid my sincere and loving attachment to them. It carries me off to quiet places, among good and simple people such as those I once knew. It reminds me of my youth and my innocent pleasures, it allows me to enjoy them anew, and very often it makes me happy even now, amidst the most miserable fate ever endured by mortal man.

EIGHTH WALK

MEDITATING on my state of mind in all the various circumstances of my life, I am extremely struck by the lack of proportion between the ups and downs of my fate and the general feelings of well-being or dejection they have aroused in me. The various periods of short-lived prosperity that I have enjoyed have left me with almost no agreeable memories of deep and lasting impressions: by contrast, in all the hardships of my life I was invariably full of affectionate, touching and delightful emotions which poured a healing balm over the wounds of my injured soul and seemed to change its pains into pleasures, and it is the sweet memory of these feelings that returns to me, unaccompanied by that of the adversities which I experienced at the same time. It seems to me that I enjoyed the pleasure of existence more completely and that I lived more fully when my emotions were so to speak concentrated around my heart by my destiny and could not go spreading themselves over all the things prized by men, things that are of so little value in themselves, though they form the sole occupation of the people we regard as happy.

When all was in order round about me and I was happy with everything surrounding me and with the sphere in which I had to live, I filled it with my affections. My expansive soul spread to encompass other objects, and I was all the time transported outside myself by a thousand different tastes and by pleasing attachments which kept my heart constantly occupied, so that I could be said to have forgotten myself. My entire being was in things that were foreign to me, and in the continual agitation of my heart I felt all the instability of human life. This stormy life gave me neither inward peace nor outward repose. Happy to all appearances, I had not a single feeling which could stand the test of thought and with which I could feel entirely at ease. I was never completely satisfied with others or with myself. I was deafened by the tumult of the world and bored by solitude, I was always wanting to move and never happy anywhere. And yet I was acclaimed, made much of, and welcomed with open arms. I had not a single enemy, no one who was malevolently or enviously disposed towards me. Since people's one concern was to shower favours on me, I often had the pleasure of doing favours in my turn, and to a great many people, so that with neither possessions, nor a position in the world, nor a patron, nor any great abilities that had had time to develop or become known, I enjoyed the advantages attached to such things and could see no one either above or below me whose situation I envied. What then did I need to make me happy? I do not know, but I know that I was not happy. And what is missing now to make me the most unfortunate of men? Nothing that mankind could do. Yet even so, in these deplorable circumstances, I would not change places with the most fortunate of my fellow-men, and I would rather be myself with all my misfortunes than one of them in all his prosperity. Reduced to my own self, it is true that I feed on my own substance, but this does not diminish and I can be self-sufficient even though I have to ruminate as it were on nothing, and though my dried-up imagination and inactive mind no longer provide my heart with any nourishment. My soul, darkened and encumbered by my bodily organs, sinks daily beneath their weight; bowed under this heavy burden, it no longer has the strength to soar as once it did above this old integument.

Adversity forces us to draw in on ourselves in this way, and this is perhaps what makes it most difficult to bear for most people. For my part, since I have only errors to reproach myself with, I can console myself by blaming them on my weakness, for premeditated evil never came near my heart.

Nevertheless, short of being totally insensible, how is it possible to contemplate my situation for a single instant without seeing how horrible they have made it, without dying of grief and despair? On the contrary, I, the most sensitive of beings, contemplate it unmoved, and without having to struggle or force myself, I can look on my situation with near-indifference when hardly anyone else could consider it without being appalled.

How has this come about? For I was far removed from this peaceful frame of mind when I first came to suspect the plot in which I had long been unwittingly ensnared. I was overwhelmed by this new discovery. The infamy and treachery of it took me by surprise. What honest soul is prepared for sufferings of this kind? To be able to foresee them, one would need to have deserved them. I fell into all the pits that had been dug for me. Indignation, fury and frenzy took possession of me. I lost my bearings. My wits were unsettled, and in the horrible darkness in which they have kept me buried, I could see no light to guide me, no support or foothold to keep me upright and help me to resist the despair that was engulfing me.

How could one live a quiet and happy life in such circumstances? Yet the circumstances have not changed, or they have changed for the worse, and I have regained my peace and tranquillity and lead a quiet and happy life in the midst of them, laughing at the incredible tortures my persecutors are constantly inflicting on themselves while I live in peace, busy with flowers, stamens and such childish things, and never giving them a moment's thought.

How did this change take place? By a natural, imperceptible and painless process. The initial shock was terrible. I, who felt myself worthy of affection and respect, who thought

myself honoured and loved as I deserved to be, suddenly
found myself disguised as an unheard of and fearful monster.
I saw a whole generation all rush headlong into this strange
belief, without explanation, doubt or shame, and without my
even being able to discover the cause of this extraordinary
turn of events. I struggled violently and succeeded only in
enmeshing myself still further. I tried to force my persecutors
to have it out with me in public; they took good care to do no
such thing. After tormenting myself for a long time, I was
bound to stop and draw breath. But I still hoped: I said to
myself: 'The whole of the human race can never be infected
by this idiotic blindness, this absurd prejudice. There are
sensible people who do not share in this madness; there are
equitable souls who detest treachery and deceit. Let me look, I
shall perhaps finish by finding a man, and if I find one, they
will all be confounded.' I sought in vain; I did not find one
single man. It is a universal league, irrevocable and without
exception, and I can be certain of ending my days in this
terrible ostracism without ever unravelling the mystery.

It is in this deplorable situation that after years of anguish I
have escaped from the despair which seemed to be my ulti-
mate lot, and recovered my serenity, tranquillity, peace and
even happiness, since every day of my life brings a pleasurable
recollection of the last and no desire for anything different in
the one to come.

What has brought about this change? One thing and one
thing only: I have learned to bear the yoke of necessity without complaining. Where previously I strove to cling on to a
host of things, now, when I have lost hold of them all one
after another and have nothing left but myself, I have at last
regained a firm footing. Under pressure from all sides, I
remain upright because I cling to nothing and lean only on
myself.

When I used to protest so fiercely against public opinion, I was still its slave without realizing it. We want to be respected by those whom we respect, and as long as I thought well of men, or at least of certain men, I could not remain indifferent to their opinion of me. I saw that the judgements of the public are often fair, but I did not see that this very fairness is often the work of chance, that the criteria on which men base their opinions are merely the fruit of their passions or of the prejudices which spring from these passions, and that even when they judge correctly, this often has an unjust cause, as when they pretend to honour the merits of a successful man not out of fairness, but to give themselves an appearance of impartiality, while they are quite prepared to slander this same person in other ways.

But when after a long and fruitless search I saw that they all without exception remained attached to the most iniquitous and absurd theory that a spirit from Hell could ever have invented, when I saw that where I was concerned reason was banished from every mind and justice from every heart, when I saw a frenzied generation give itself over entirely to the blind fury of its leaders against an unfortunate individual who never harmed anyone, never wished anyone ill and never rendered evil for evil, when after vainly seeking a man I had finally to put out my lantern[1] exclaiming: 'There is not a single one left,' then I began to see that I was alone in the world, and I understood that my contemporaries acted towards me like automata, entirely governed by external impulses, and that I could only calculate their behaviour according to the laws of motion. Any intention or passion that I might have supposed them to possess could never have provided an intelligible explanation of their conduct towards me. Thus it was that their inner feelings ceased to matter to

1. A reference to Diogenes who was supposed to have gone about with a lantern in search of a man. Rousseau liked to use this parallel in his later years.

me; I came to see them as no more than bodies endowed with different movements, but devoid of any moral relation to me.

In all the ills that befall us, we are more concerned by the intention than the result. A tile that falls off a roof may injure us more seriously, but it will not wound us so deeply as a stone thrown deliberately by a malevolent hand. The blow may miss, but the intention always strikes home. The physical pain is what we feel least of all when fortune assails us, and when suffering people do not know whom to blame for their misfortunes, they attribute them to a destiny, and personify this destiny, lending it eyes and a mind that takes pleasure in tormenting them. In the same way a gambler who is angered by his losses will fly into a fury against some unknown enemy; he imagines a fate which deliberately persists in torturing him, and having found something to feed his anger on, he storms and rages against the enemy that he has himself created. The wise man sees in all his misfortunes no more than the blows of blind necessity and feels none of this senseless agitation; his pain makes him cry out, but without anger or exasperation, he feels only the physical impact of the evil that besets him, and though the blows may hurt his body, not one of them can touch his heart.

To have come so far is excellent, but it is not enough if one stops there. That would be like cutting down the evil, but leaving the root in the ground, for this root is not in beings outside us, but in ourselves, and that is where we must exert ourselves to pull it out completely. This became obvious to me when once I had begun to be myself again. Since by the light of reason I could see nothing but absurdities in the explanations I tried to give for everything that happened to me, I realized that, as all its causes and operations were unknown and incomprehensible to me, I should ignore them completely, that I should regard all the details of my fate as the workings of mere necessity, in which I should not seek to find any intention, purpose, or moral cause, that I must submit to it without argument or resistance since these were useless, that since all that was left to me on earth was to regard myself as a purely passive being, I should not waste the strength I needed to endure my fate in trying to fight against it. This was what I told myself. My reason and my heart assented, yet I could feel that my heart was not entirely satisfied. Whence came this dissatisfaction? I searched and found the answer: it came from my self-love, which, having waxed indignant against mankind, still rebelled against reason.

This discovery was not as easy as one might believe, for an innocent and persecuted man is all too inclined to mistake his own petty pride for a pure love of justice, but on the other hand, once the real cause is found, it is easy to remedy, or at least to deflect to another course. Self-esteem is the strongest impulse of proud souls; self-love, with its train of illusions, can often creep in under the guise of self-esteem, but when the fraud is finally revealed and self-love can no longer conceal itself, there is no further cause to fear it, and though it may be hard to destroy, at least it is easy to subdue.

I was never much given to self-love; but in the world this artificial passion has been exacerbated in me, particularly when I was a writer; I may perhaps have had less of it than my fellow-authors, but it was still excessive. The terrible lessons I received quickly reduced it to its original proportions. At first it rebelled against injustice, but in the end it came to treat it with contempt; falling back on my own soul, severing the external links which make it so demanding, and giving up all ideas of comparison or precedence, it was content that I be good in my own eyes. And so, becoming once again the proper love of self,[2] it returned to the true natural order and freed me from the tyranny of public opinion.

2. On the important distinction between 'self-love' and 'love of self' see the Introduction, p. 19.

From this time on I recovered my peace of mind and something akin to happiness. Whatever our situation, it is only self-love that can make us constantly unhappy. When it is silent and we listen to the voice of reason, this can console us in the end for all the misfortunes which it was not in our power to avoid. Indeed it makes them disappear, in so far as they have no immediate effect on us, for one can be sure of avoiding their worst buffets by ceasing to take any notice of them. They are as nothing to the person who ignores them. Insults, reprisals, offences, injuries, injustices are all nothing to the man who sees in the hardships he suffers nothing but the hardships themselves and not the intention behind them, and whose place in his own self-esteem does not depend on the good-will of others. However men choose to regard me, they cannot change my essential being, and for all their power and all their secret plots I shall continue, whatever they do, to be what I am in spite of them. It is true that their attitude towards me has an influence on my material situation. The wall they have set up between us robs me of every source of subsistence or assistance in my old age and my time of need. It makes even money useless to me, since money cannot buy the help I need, and there is no intercourse, no mutual aid, no communication between us. Alone in their midst, I have only myself to fall back on, and this is a feeble support at my age and in my situation. These are great misfortunes, but they are no longer so painful to me now that I have learned to endure them patiently. There are not many things that we really need. Forethought and imagination multiply their number, and it is these unceasing cares which make us anxious and unhappy. But I, even if I know that I shall suffer tomorrow, can be content as long as I am not suffering today. I am not affected by the ills I foresee, but only by those I feel, and this reduces them to very little. Solitary, sick, and left alone in my bed, I could die there of poverty, cold and hunger without anyone caring. But what does it matter if I myself do not care and am no more affected than the rest of them by my fate, whatever it may be? Is it such a small achievement, particularly at my age, to have learned to regard life and death, sickness and health, riches and poverty, fame and slander with equal indifference? All other old men worry about everything, nothing worries me. Whatever may happen, I do not care, and this indifference is not the work of my own wisdom, it is that of my enemies and compensates me for the evils they inflict upon me. In making me insensible to adversity they have done me more good than if they had spared me its blows. If I did not experience it I might still fear it, but now that I have subdued it I have no more cause to fear.

In the midst of my afflictions this disposition gives free rein to my natural nonchalance almost as completely as if I were living in the most total prosperity. Apart from the brief moments when the objects around me recall my most painful anxieties, all the rest of the time, following the promptings of my natural affections, my heart continues to feed on the emotions for which it was created, and I enjoy them together with the imaginary beings who provoke them and share them with me, just as if those beings really existed. They exist for me, their creator, and I have no fear that they will betray or abandon me; they will last as long as my misfortunes and will suffice to make me forget them.

Everything brings me back to the sweet and happy life for which I was born; I spend three-quarters of my life either busy with instructive and even pleasant objects, to which it is a joy to devote my mind and my senses, or with the children of my imagination, the creatures of my heart's desire, whose presence satisfies its yearnings, or else alone with myself, contented with myself and already enjoying the happiness which I feel I have deserved. Love of self alone is active in all of this, self-love has no part in it. The same is not true during those unhappy moments which I still spend among men, a plaything of their Judas kisses, their extravagant and hollow compliments and their honeyed malice. For all my efforts, self-love steps in on such occasions. I suffer agonies from the hate and animosity I see in their hearts under such crude disguises, and in addition to this pain the idea of being duped in such a silly way causes me a childish resentment, the product of a foolish self-love whose stupidity I can see all too clearly without being able to suppress it. The efforts I have made to harden myself against these insulting and mocking looks are unbelievable. A hundred times I have walked in public places and on the busiest thoroughfares with the sole object of learning to put up with these cruel looks; not only was I unable to do so, I did not even make any progress and all my painful and fruitless efforts left me just as vulnerable as before to being upset, hurt or exasperated.

Governed by my senses whether I like it or not, I have never been able to resist the impressions they make on me, and as long as they are affected by some object my heart remains equally affected, but this passing emotion lasts no longer than the sensations that cause it. The presence of people who hate me affects me violently, but as soon as they disappear the emotion ceases; out of sight, out of mind. Even when I know that they are going to concern themselves with me, I am unable to concern myself with them. The suffering which I no longer actually feel has not the slightest effect on me; the persecutor whom I cannot see is as nothing to me. I can see what an advantage this gives to those who control my destiny. Let them control it as they please. I would rather be exposed to all their torments than be obliged to think about them in order to protect myself from their attacks.

This influence of my senses on my heart is my one torment in life. On the days when I see no one, I give no thought to my fate, I am no longer conscious of it and I do not suffer; I live happy and contented with nothing to distract or hinder me. But it is not often that I can avoid all painful impressions, and when such things are furthest from my mind I notice some gesture or sinister look, overhear some barbed remark or meet some malicious person, and this is enough to upset me completely. All I can do in such circumstances is to forget as quickly as I can and run away. The turmoil in my heart vanishes with the object that has caused it and calm descends on my soul again as soon as I am alone. Or if anything does worry me, it is the fear of meeting some new cause of suffering. This is my only source of distress, but it is enough to spoil my happiness. I live in the middle of Paris. When I leave my home, I long for solitude and the country, but they are so far away that before I can breathe freely I have to encounter a thousand things that oppress my heart, and half the day goes by in anguish before I reach the refuge I am looking for. Indeed, I am lucky to be allowed to get there. The moment when I escape from the horde of evil-doers is one of joy, and as soon as I am under the trees and surrounded by greenery, I feel as if I were in the earthly paradise and experience an inward pleasure as intense as if I were the happiest of men.

I well remember how in my brief periods of prosperity these same solitary walks which give me such pleasure today were tedious and insipid to me. When I was staying with someone in the country the need for exercise and fresh air often led me to go walking by myself, and I would sneak out like a thief and wander through the park or the countryside, but far from enjoying the quiet happiness that I find there today, I took with me the turmoil of futile ideas which had occupied me in the salon; the memory of the company I had left followed me in my solitude, the fumes of self-love and the bustle of the world dimmed the freshness of the groves in my eyes and troubled my secluded peace. Though I fled into the depths of the woods, an importunate crowd followed me everywhere and came between me and Nature. Only when I had detached myself from the social passions and their dismal train did I find her once again in all her beauty.

Convinced of the impossibility of repressing these first involuntary reactions, I have given up the attempt. Whenever I am provoked, I allow my blood to boil and my senses to be possessed by anger and indignation; I give way to this first explosion of nature, which all my efforts could not prevent or impede. I merely try to stop it leading to any undesirable consequences. My eyes flash, my face flares up, my limbs tremble and palpitations choke me; these are all purely physical reactions and reasoning has no effect on them, but once nature has had this initial explosion one can become one's own master again and gradually regain control over one's senses; this is what I have tried to do, for a long time to no avail, but eventually with greater success. And instead of wasting my efforts on pointless resistance, I wait for the moment when I can achieve victory by appealing to my reason, for it only speaks when it can make itself heard. Alas! What am I saying? My reason? It would be quite wrong of me to attribute this victory to reason, for it has little to do with it; all my behaviour is equally the work of a volatile temperament which is stirred up by violent winds but calms down as soon as the winds stop blowing; it is the ardour of my character that excites me and the nonchalance of my character that pacifies me. I give way to the impulse of the moment; every shock sets up a vigorous and short lived motion in me, but as soon as the shock is over the motion vanishes, and nothing that comes from outside can be prolonged within me. All the vicissitudes of fortune and the stratagems of men can have little hold on a man of my kind. For the suffering to last the external cause would have to be constantly renewed, because any interval, however short, is enough for me to regain my self-control. I am at men's mercy as long as they can act on my senses, but they have only to grant me a moment's respite for me to revert to my natural state; whatever men may do, this is my most enduring state and the one in which, in spite of destiny, I enjoy the kind of happiness for which I feel I was made. I have described this state in one of my reveries. It suits me so well that I desire nothing other than that it should continue and never be disturbed. The evil that men have done me does not affect me in the least; only the fear of what they may still do to me is capable of disquieting me, but being certain that there is no new hold which they can use to inflict some permanent suffering on me, I laugh at all their scheming and enjoy my own existence in spite of them.

NINTH WALK

HAPPINESS is a lasting state which does not seem to be made for man in this world. Everything here on earth is in a continual flux which allows nothing to assume any constant form. All things change round about us, we ourselves change, and no one can be sure of loving tomorrow what he loves today. All our plans of happiness in this life are therefore empty dreams. Let us make the most of peace of mind when it comes to us, taking care to do nothing to drive it away, but not making plans to hold it fast, since such plans are sheer folly. I have seen few if any happy people, but I have seen many who were contented, and of all the sights that have come my way this is the one that has left me most contented myself. I think this is a natural consequence of the influence of my sensations on my inward feelings. Happiness cannot be detected by any outward sign and to recognize it one would need to be able to read in the happy person's heart, but contentment is visible in the eyes, the bearing, the voice and the walk, and it seems to communicate itself to the onlooker. Is there any satisfaction more sweet than to see a whole people devoting themselves to joy on some feast-day and all their hearts expanding in the supreme rays of pleasure which shine briefly but intensely through the clouds of life?

Three days ago I had a visit from Monsieur P., who was extraordinarily anxious to show me Monsieur d'Alembert's obituary of Madame Geoffrin.[1] Before reading it, he roared with laughter for some time at its ridiculous air of novelty and the many trifling plays on words which he said it contained.

1. Patron to many Parisian writers of the time; died on 6 October 1777. D'Alembert was a famous mathematician, co-editor of the *Encyclopedia* and Secretary of the French Academy.

He was still laughing when he began to read, but I listened to him with a serious face which calmed him down, and seeing that I was not following his example, he finally stopped laughing. The longest and most elaborate part of the obituary concerned the pleasure Madame Geoffrin took in seeing children and engaging them in conversation; the author rightly gave this inclination as proof of a good character. But he did not stop there, and unhesitatingly accused all those who did not share this taste of having a bad character and a hard heart, going so far as to claim that if everyone who was being taken to be hanged or broken on the wheel was questioned on this point, they would all admit to not having loved children. These assertions produced an odd effect in their context. Even supposing them all to be true, was this the time to make them, and was it right to disfigure the obituary of a good woman with these images of torture and crime? I had no difficulty in detecting the motive behind this unpleasant show of concern, and after Monsieur P. had finished reading I not only praised the parts of the obituary which had impressed me, but added that the author had felt more hate than love in his heart when he wrote it.

The next day being quite fine, though cold, I took a walk as far as the Military Academy, expecting to find some mosses in full flower there. On my way I wondered about the previous day's visit and the piece by Monsieur d'Alembert, in which I was pretty sure that this irrelevant passage had not been included to no purpose; the mere eagerness to show me this brochure when usually everything is kept from me, made it clear enough what this purpose was. I had put my children in the Foundlings' Home, and this was enough for people to misrepresent me as an unnatural father, and so, developing this idea and embroidering on it, they had gradually reached the obvious conclusion that I hated children; as I followed this progression of ideas, I wondered at the art with which human ingenuity manages to turn white into black. For I do not believe that any man has ever loved seeing little children romping and playing together more than I do, and I often stop in the street or on the boulevards to look at their little tricks and games with an interest which no one else seems to share. The very day that Monsieur P. came to see me, I had had a visit an hour earlier from the two little Du Soussoi's, my landlord's younger children, the older of whom is about seven; they had been so ready to come and embrace me, and I had returned their caresses so affectionately, that in spite of the difference in age they had seemed truly to enjoy being with me, and for my part I was overjoyed to see that my old face had not repelled them – indeed the younger boy seemed to come back so willingly to see me that I was more childish than the children and felt especially attached to him, feeling as much regret when he went as if he had been my own son.

I can understand that the reproach of having put my children in the Foundlings' Home should easily have degenerated, with a little embellishment, into that of being an unnatural father and a child-hater. Nevertheless there is no doubt that in doing so I was influenced most of all by the fear that any other course of action would almost inevitably bring upon them a fate a thousand times worse. Had I been less concerned about what would happen to them, since I was not in a position to bring them up myself, I should have been obliged by my circumstances to leave their education to their mother, who would have spoiled them, and to her family, who would have made monsters of them. What Mahomet did to Séide[2] would have been as nothing compared to what would have been done to them with regard to me, and the traps that have subsequently been laid for me in this connection are confirmation enough of the plot that was hatched at this time. It

2. In Voltaire's tragedy *Mahomet* the young Séide is persuaded by Mahomet's teaching to kill his own father.

is true that in those days I was far from foreseeing these terrible schemes, but I knew that the least dangerous form of education they could have was at the Foundlings' Home, so I put them there. I should do the same thing again with even fewer misgivings if the choice were still before me, and I am sure that no father is more affectionate than I would have been towards them once habit had had time to reinforce my natural inclination.

If I have made any progress in the knowledge of the human heart, I owe it to the pleasure I took in seeing and observing children. This same pleasure was something of an obstacle to progress in my youth, for I played with children so gaily and enthusiastically that I hardly thought to study them. But noticing with advancing years that my antique appearance frightened them, I stopped bothering them, preferring to deprive myself of a pleasure rather than disturb their happiness; contenting myself thereafter with watching their games and all their little ways. I found a compensation for my sacrifice in the light which these observations shed on the true and original impulses of nature, which are a closed book to all our men of science. My writings are there to prove that I engaged in this study with the attentive care of someone who enjoyed his work, and it would surely be the most incredible thing if *Julie* and *Émile* were the work of a man who did not like children.

I never possessed any presence of mind or ease of speech, but since my misfortunes my tongue and my head have become increasingly slow and confused. I can find neither the ideas nor the words I want, and nothing calls for a clearer head and a more careful choice of words than talking to children. What makes things even worse for me is the presence of attentive onlookers, the importance they attach and the interpretations they give to everything said by someone who has written specifically for children and is therefore supposed to utter nothing but oracles when talking to them. This extreme awkwardness and the awareness of my incompetence embarrasses and disconcerts me, and I should be more at home meeting some Asiatic potentate than getting a little child to chat with me.

There is another drawback which keeps me away from them more than before, with the result that since the beginning of my misfortunes, although I still enjoy seeing them as much as ever, I am no longer on such familiar terms with them. Children do not like old age, they are repelled by the appearance of nature on the decline; it hurts me deeply to see this and I prefer to refrain from caressing them rather than embarrass or repel them. Only truly loving souls can ever feel this reluctance, which is unknown to all our learned gentlemen and blue-stockings. Little did Madame Geoffrin care if children enjoyed her company, so long as she enjoyed theirs. But for me the pleasure is worse than non-existent, it is negative unless it is shared, and I am no longer of an age or situation in which I can see children's little hearts at ease with mine. If this were still possible, the pleasure would be all the keener for its infrequency – and this is indeed what I discovered the other morning from the pleasure given me by my affectionate chat with the little Du Soussoi's, not only because the maid accompanying them did not greatly intimidate me and I felt less of a need to watch my step in her presence, but because they kept the same cheerful appearance they had on greeting me and did not seem to find my company tedious or disagreeable.

Oh, if I could still enjoy some of those moments of pure and heartfelt affection, even if only from a little child, if I could still see in someone's eyes the joy and satisfaction of being with me, how these brief but happy effusions of the heart would compensate me for my many troubles and afflictions! No longer should I have to seek among animals the kind looks that humanity now refuses me! I can only judge from very few examples, but these are dear to my memory. Here is one, which in any other circumstances I should have almost entirely forgotten; the impression it made on me is a clear indication of my miserable state.

Two years ago, having gone for a walk by Nouvelle France,[3] I carried on beyond it and then, going off to the left with the intention of making a circuit of Montmartre, I passed through the village of Clignancourt. I was walking along dreamily and absent-mindedly without looking about me, when suddenly I felt someone tugging at my knees. I looked down and saw a little child of five or six, who was hugging my knees with all his might and looking at me with such a friendly and affectionate air that it touched me to the quick. That is how my children would have treated me, I thought. I picked up the child in my arms, kissed him several times in a kind of rapture and then went on my way. As I walked on, I felt that something was missing, that there was some growing desire urging me to turn back; I blamed myself for leaving the child so suddenly, and imagined I detected in this apparently unmotivated act a sort of inspiration that I ought not to disregard. Finally I gave way to temptation, turned back and, running to the child, embraced him again, gave him money to buy some Nanterre rolls which a passing salesman happened to have, and started him chattering. I asked him who his father was, and he pointed to a man who was hooping a barrel. I was about to leave the child and go over to talk to him, when I saw that I had been forestalled by a supicious-looking individual who looked to me like one of the spies who are kept constantly on my trail; as this man whispered to him, I saw the cooper begin staring at me with a look which was anything but friendly. This sight immediately damped my emotions, and I left the father and child even

3. A hamlet about a mile from Saint-Lazare.

more rapidly than I had returned to them, but in a much less agreeable agitation which altered my whole state of mind.

Even so, I have quite often experienced the same feeling since then and have several times walked through Clignancourt in the hope of seeing the child, but I have never again seen either him or his father, and all that remains of this encounter is a quite vivid memory tinged always with affection and sadness like all the emotions that still occasionally touch my heart.

Everything has its compensations; if my pleasures are brief and few in number, it is also true that when they come they give me an intenser enjoyment than if I were more used to them. I ruminate on them so to speak, turning them over frequently in my memory, and few as they are, if they were pure and unmixed, they would perhaps make me happier than in my days of prosperity. In extreme poverty a little is enough to make one rich; a beggar is gladder to find one gold coin than a rich man to find a purse full of money. People would laugh if they could see how my soul is affected by the slightest pleasures of this kind, when I can conceal them from the vigilance of my persecutors. One of the most delightful of these happenings occurred some four or five years ago, and I cannot recall it without feeling a thrill of pleasure at having made such good use of it.

One Sunday my wife and I had gone to have dinner at the Porte Maillot. After dinner we walked across the Bois de Boulogne as far as La Muette;[4] there we sat down on the grass in the shade waiting for the sun to go down a little before returning gently home by way of Passy. A group of about twenty little girls escorted by a sort of religious sister came and settled themselves quite close to us, some sitting down and others frolicking about. While they were playing, a

4. The splendid gardens of the Château de la Muette lay close to the Bois de Boulogne, about a mile west of Passy.

wafer-seller came by with his drum and his wheel looking for customers to try their luck. I could see that the little girls were looking longingly at the wafers, and two or three of them, who apparently had a few coppers, asked if they could buy a ticket. While their governess was hesitating and arguing with them I called the man over and told him: 'Let all these young ladies draw tickets in turn and I will pay for the lot.' These words filled the whole company with a joy which would have been worth more than all the money in my purse, if it had cost me so much.

Seeing that they were rushing up in some disorder, I obtained their governess's permission to make them all line up on one side and then go over to the other side one by one as they drew their tickets. Although there were no blank tickets so that everyone had at least one wafer and no one could be completely disappointed, I wanted to make things even more festive and secretly told the man to use his customary skill in a different way from usual and make as many lucky numbers come up as he could, promising to make it worth his while. Thanks to this stratagem nearly a hundred wafers were distributed, even though none of the girls drew more than one ticket, for in this respect I was inexorable, not wanting to give rise to abuses or show any favouritism which might cause discontent. My wife got the lucky ones to share with the others so that almost everyone received the same number and there was general rejoicing.

I asked the sister if she would draw a ticket too, though I was very much afraid that she might scorn my offer; she accepted it with a good grace, drew a ticket like her charges and took her winnings unaffectedly. I felt very grateful to her for this, and it seemed to me that her acceptance showed a very attractive politeness, which is worth any amount of affected airs and grimaces. Throughout this whole operation there were disputes which were brought to my judgement seat, and as these little girls came one by one to plead their causes I had occasion to observe that although none of them was pretty, the pleasant ways of some of them made one forget their plainness.

We eventually parted company very pleased with each other, and in all my life that afternoon is one of the ones I re-member with the greatest satisfaction. Nor did the festivities drain my purse; I spent thirty sous in all, and it brought me several hundred francs' worth of happiness, so true is it that genuine pleasure is not to be measured by what it costs and that joy goes better with copper than with gold. I have often returned to the same place at the same hour, hoping to meet the little band there again, but I have never been in luck.

This reminds me of another amusement of much the same sort which I remember from much further back. It was in those unhappy days when I mixed with the rich and the men of letters and was sometimes reduced to taking part in their miserable pleasures. I was at La Chevrette[5] for the name-day of the master of the house; his whole family had gathered to celebrate it, and to this end they brought out the whole brilliant array of noisy pleasures. Games, theatricals, banquets, fireworks, nothing was spared. There was no time to draw breath and the effect was stunning rather than entertaining. After dinner we went out to take the air in the avenue. A kind of fair was going on there. There was dancing; the gentlemen condescended to dance with the peasant girls, but the ladies remained aloof. Gingerbread was being sold. A young man in the company had the idea of buying some and throwing the pieces one by one into the thick of the crowd, and every-one was so pleased to see all the yokels rushing, fighting and knocking one another down so as to get hold of a piece that

5. A country house belonging to Madame d'Epinay, one of the group of Encyclopedists. Rousseau had lived as her tenant in the near-by Hermitage in 1756-7. See the *Confessions*, Book 9.

they all wanted to join in the fun. So pieces of gingerbread went flying in all directions and girls and boys rushed about, piling on top of one another and crippling themselves; everybody thought it a quite charming sight. Out of embarrassment I did the same as all the rest, although inwardly I did not find it as amusing as they did. But soon, growing weary of emptying my purse to have people crushed, I abandoned the fine company and went walking by myself through the fair. The variety of different sights kept me amused for a long time. Among other things I saw five or six urchins gathered round a little girl who still had a dozen or so pathetic little apples on her stall that she would have been only too happy to sell. The boys too would very much have liked to help her get rid of them, but they had only a few coppers between them, and this was not enough to make great inroads into the apples. The stall was a Garden of the Hesperides for them, and the little girl the dragon that guarded it. This comic scene amused me for quite some time, but I finally provided a *dénouement* by buying the apples from the little girl and letting her share them out among the little boys. Then I had one of the sweetest sights which the human heart can enjoy, that of seeing joy and youthful innocence all around me, for the spectators too had a part in the emotion that met their eyes and I, who shared in this joy at so little cost to myself, had the added pleasure of feeling that I was the author of it.

When I compared this entertainment with those I had just left behind, I had the satisfaction of feeling the difference which separates healthy tastes and natural pleasures from those that spring from opulence and are hardly more than pleasures of mockery and exclusive tastes founded on disdain. For what sort of pleasure could one derive from seeing herds of men degraded by poverty crowding together, suffocating and brutally crushing one another in the greedy struggle for a few hunks of gingerbread which had been trampled underfoot and covered in mud?

For my part, when I have thought deeply about the sort of pleasure I enjoyed on such occasions, I have found that it consists less in the consciousness of doing good than in the joy of seeing happy faces. This sight has a charm for me which, although it may touch my heart, still comes entirely from my sensations. When I do not see the pleasure I cause, even if there is no doubt about it, I am robbed of half my enjoyment. Indeed this is for me a disinterested pleasure which is independent of the part I play in it, for I have always been very attracted by the pleasure of seeing cheerful faces in popular rejoicings. This expectation has often been thwarted in France, however, for this nation which claims to be so cheerful shows little of this cheerfulness in its recreations. At one time I often went to cafés to see poor people dancing, but their dances were so dreary and the dancers looked so miserable and awkward that I used to come away more depressed than heartened by the sight. But in Geneva and Switzerland, where laughter is not continually dissipated in malicious fooling, holidays have an air of contentment and cheerfulness, poverty does not show its hideous face, nor does pomp flaunt its insolence; well-being, fraternity and concord open all hearts to one another and often in the transports of innocent joy strangers accost one another, embrace and invite one another to join together in enjoying the day's pleasures. In order to enjoy these charming festivities myself, I have no need to be taking part in them, I only need to see them; this is enough to give me a share in them, and among all these cheerful faces I can be certain that there is no heart more cheerful than mine.

Although this pleasure springs entirely from sensation, it certainly has a moral cause, and the proof of this is that the same sight, instead of pleasing and delighting me, can fill me with agonies of pain and indignation when I know that these signs of pleasure on the faces of evil-doers are nothing but signs that their malice is satisfied. Innocent joy is the only joy whose appearance delights my heart. The appearance of cruel or mocking joy wounds and distresses it, even if it has nothing to do with me. No doubt the signs cannot be exactly the same in both cases, since they spring from such different causes, but even so they are all signs of joy and the visible difference between them is certainly not proportionate to the difference between the emotions they excite in me.

The marks of pain and grief affect me still more, so much so that I cannot endure them without myself being stirred by emotions which are perhaps even more intense than those they express. Imagination joins forces with sensation and makes me identify myself with the sufferer, often plunging me in greater distress than he himself feels. A discontented face is another sight that I cannot bear, particularly when I have reason to believe that this discontent concerns me. I cannot tell how much gold was extracted from me by the grumpy and glum faces of valets doing unwilling service in the houses where I was once foolish enough to let myself be dragged, and where the servants always made me pay dearly for the masters' hospitality. Always too strongly affected by what I see or hear, and particularly by signs of pleasure or suffering, affection or dislike, I let myself be swayed by these outward impressions and can only avoid them by running away. A sign, a gesture or a glance from a stranger is enough to disturb my pleasure or ease my suffering. It is only when I am alone that I am my own master, at all other times I am the plaything of all who surround me.

I used once to enjoy living in society, when I saw only friendship in all eyes, or at worst indifference in the eyes of those to whom I was a stranger. But today, when as much care is taken to make my face known to people as to disguise my true nature, I cannot set foot in the street without being immediately surrounded by distressing sights. I make off as quickly as I can into the country, and as soon as I see the green leaves I begin to breathe freely. Is it surprising that I love solitude? I see nothing but animosity in the faces of men, and nature always smiles on me.

Nevertheless I must admit that I still feel pleasure in living among men as long as my face is unknown to them. But this is a pleasure which I am hardly ever allowed to enjoy. A few years ago I still liked walking through villages and seeing the men mending their flails in the morning or the women with their children at the cottage doors. There was something in this sight that touched my heart; sometimes I stopped unthinkingly to watch these people at their little tasks and felt myself sighing without knowing why. I do not know whether seeing that I was affected by this little pleasure gave my enemies the desire to take it away from me too, but the change I can see on people's faces as I go past and the new way they look at me make it quite obvious that someone has taken steps to remove my incognito. The same thing has happened to me at the Invalides[6] in an even more striking way. I have always felt an interest in this noble establishment. I can never look without emotion and veneration at the groups of good old men who can say like those of Sparta:

> We have been in former days
> Young and valiant and brave.

One of my favourite walks was around the Military Academy, and I used to have the pleasure of meeting here and there some of the old pensioners who still retained the old military courtesy and saluted me as I went by. This salute, which my heart returned to them a hundred-fold, delighted me and added to the pleasure I felt in seeing them. Being unable to conceal

6. A hospital for veteran soldiers.

anything that affects me, I often talked about these pensioners and said how touched I was to see them. That was all that was needed. Some time later I noticed that I was no longer a stranger to them, or rather that I was much more of a stranger, since they gave me the same sort of looks as the general public. No more courtesy, no more salutes. An unfriendly air and an unwelcoming look had taken the place of their earliest politeness. Since the sincerity belonging to their former profession does not allow them to do like everyone else and conceal their animosity under a sneering and treacherous mask, they openly display the most violent hate towards me, and so extreme is my misfortune that I am obliged to give the first place in my esteem to those who least disguise their fury.

Since this change I have taken less pleasure in walking by the Invalides, but as my feelings towards them do not depend on how they regard me, I can never contemplate these former defenders of their country without respect and affection; but I find it very hard to be so poorly repaid for the justice I do them. When I happen to meet one of them who has escaped the general instruction or who, not knowing my face, displays no aversion to me, the courteous salute I receive from this one man makes up for the hostile attitude of all the rest. I forget about them and think only of him, and I imagine that he has a soul like mine, a soul impervious to hate. I had this pleasure as recently as last year, when I was crossing the Seine to go walking on the Île des Cygnes.[7] A poor old pensioner was waiting in a boat for someone to cross with him. I stepped in and told the waterman to begin rowing. There was a strong current and the crossing was a long one. I dared hardly speak to the pensioner for fear of being insulted and rebuffed as usual, but his courteous appearance reassured me. We

7. This island used to stretch between the Trocadéro and the Invalides; it was joined to the Left Bank of the Seine early in the nineteenth century.

chatted. He seemed a sensible and decent man. I was surprised and delighted by his frank and affable manner. I was not used to such kind treatment, and my surprise ceased when I discovered that he had only just arrived from the provinces. I realized that he had not yet been taught my face and given his instructions. I took advantage of my incognito to have a few moments of conversation with a man, and the happiness this gave me made me feel how even the most common pleasures acquire a new value from being rare. Stepping out of the boat, he was getting ready his two poor coppers. I paid for the crossing and begged him to put his money away, trembling lest he take offence. He did nothing of the kind, indeed he appeared grateful for the charity, and even more so when I helped him out of the boat, since he was older than me. Who could believe that I was so childish as to weep for joy? I was dying to press a coin into his hand so that he could buy himself some tobacco, but I did not have the courage. The same diffidence that restrained me has often prevented me from doing good deeds which would have filled me with joy, and I have often had to deplore my own feebleness in refraining from them. This time, after taking leave of my old pensioner, I quickly consoled myself with the thought that I should have been acting against my own principles, so to speak, by attaching to good deeds the sort of price which degrades their nobility and tarnishes their disinterestedness. One should hasten to help those who are in need, but in ordinary human dealings let us allow natural kindliness and sociability each to do its work without letting so pure a spring be sullied or polluted by any mercenary or venal motive. They say that in Holland the ordinary people ask to be paid for telling you the time or showing you the way; it must be a very despicable people that can buy and sell the simplest duties of humanity in this way.

I have noticed that only in Europe is hospitality put up for sale. Throughout Asia you are lodged free of charge. I know that often it is harder to find the comforts you are used to. But then it is something to be able to say to yourself: 'I am a man and I am the guest of my fellow-men; it is pure humanity that I have to thank for my sustenance.' Little hardships are easy to endure when the heart is better treated than the body.

TENTH WALK

TODAY, Palm Sunday, it is exactly fifty years since first I met Madame de Warens. She was twenty-eight then, having been born with the century. I was not yet seventeen, and all unknown to me the approach of manhood was making my naturally fervent heart burn with a new ardour. If it was not surprising that she should be kindly disposed towards a lively, yet gentle and modest young man of quite pleasing appearance, it was even less surprising that a charming, intelligent and graceful woman should make me feel not only gratitude, but more tender feelings which I was unable to distinguish from it. But what is more unusual is this: that this first impulse determined my whole life and led inexorably to the fate that has governed the rest of my days. My soul's most precious faculties had not yet been brought forth by my physical development, nor had it yet acquired a definite form. It was waiting with a kind of impatience for the moment that would shape it, but this moment, though hastened by this meeting, was not to come for a while yet, and thanks to the simple ways my education had given me I continued for a long time to live in that delightful but short-lived state where love and innocence can co-exist in one heart. She had sent me away. Everything called me back to her, I had to return. This return decided my fate, and long before I came to possess her, I lived only for her and my whole life was in hers. Ah! if only I had satisfied her heart as she satisfied mine! What peaceful and delightful days we should have spent together! We did indeed have such days, but how brief and fleeting they were, and what a fate has followed them! There is not a day when I do not remember with joy and loving emotion that one short time in my life when I was myself, completely myself, unmixed and unimpeded, and when I can genuinely claim to have lived. I can say more or less the same thing as the Pretorian Prefect who was disgraced under Vespasian and went to end his days in the country: 'I have spent seventy years on earth and I have lived for seven of them.' Were it not for that short but precious period, I should perhaps have remained uncertain about my true nature, for throughout the rest of my life, weak and unresisting, I have been so shaken, tossed and torn by the passions of others that, having remained almost passive in a life so full of storms, I should find it hard to decide what there is of my own in the conduct of my life, so unceasingly have I been oppressed by harsh necessity. But during those few years, loved by a gentle and indulgent woman, I did what I wanted, I was what I wanted, and by the use I made of my hours of leisure, helped by her teaching and example, I succeeded in imparting to my still simple and naïve soul the form which best suited it and which it has retained ever since. The taste for solitude and contemplation grew up in my heart along with the expansive and tender feelings which are best able to nourish it. Noise and turmoil constrain and quench them, peace and quiet revive and intensify them. I need tranquillity if I am to love. I persuaded Mamma to live in the country. A lonely house on a valley slope was our place of refuge, and it is there that in the space of four or five years I enjoyed a century of life and a pure and complete happiness, whose delightful memory can outweigh all that is appalling in my present fate. I needed a female friend after my own heart, and I had one. I had longed for the country, and my wish was granted. I could not bear subjection, and I was perfectly free, or better than free because I was subject only to my own affections and did only what I wanted to do. All my hours were filled with loving cares and country pursuits. I wanted nothing except that such a sweet state should never cease. My only cause of sorrow was the fear that it might not last long, and this fear, founded as it was on our precarious financial situation, was not unjustified.

From then on I attempted both to distract myself from this anxiety and to find means of preventing the realization of my fears. I decided that a rich store of talents was the surest protection against poverty, and I resolved to employ my leisure hours in making myself able if possible one day to repay the best of women for all the help she had given me.

FOR THE BEST IN PAPERBACKS, LOOK FOR THE

In every corner of the world, on every subject under the sun, Penguin represents quality and variety – the very best in publishing today.

For complete information about books available from Penguin – including Pelicans, Puffins, Peregrines and Penguin Classics – and how to order them, write to us at the appropriate address below. Please note that for copyright reasons the selection of books varies from country to country.

In the United Kingdom: For a complete list of books available from Penguin in the U.K., please write to *Dept E.P., Penguin Books Ltd, Harmondsworth, Middlesex, UB7 0DA*

In the United States: For a complete list of books available from Penguin in the U.S., please write to *Dept BA, Penguin, 299 Murray Hill Parkway, East Rutherford, New Jersey 07073*

In Canada: For a complete list of books available from Penguin in Canada, please write to *Penguin Books Canada Ltd, 2801 John Street, Markham, Ontario L3R 1B4*

In Australia: For a complete list of books available from Penguin in Australia, please write to the *Marketing Department, Penguin Books Australia Ltd, P.O. Box 257, Ringwood, Victoria 3134*

In New Zealand: For a complete list of books available from Penguin in New Zealand, please write to the *Marketing Department, Penguin Books (NZ) Ltd, Private Bag, Takapuna, Auckland 9*

In India: For a complete list of books available from Penguin, please write to *Penguin Overseas Ltd, 706 Eros Apartments, 56 Nehru Place, New Delhi, 110019*

In Holland: For a complete list of books available from Penguin in Holland, please write to *Penguin Books Nederland B.V., Postbus 195, NL–1380AD Weesp, Netherlands*

In Germany: For a complete list of books available from Penguin, please write to *Penguin Books Ltd, Friedrichstrasse 10 – 12, D–6000 Frankfurt Main 1, Federal Republic of Germany*

In Spain: For a complete list of books available from Penguin in Spain, please write to *Longman Penguin España, Calle San Nicolas 15, E–28013 Madrid, Spain*

Netochka Nezvanova   Fyodor Dostoyevsky

Dostoyevsky's first book tells the story of 'Nameless Nobody' and introduces many of the themes and issues which will dominate his great masterpieces.

Selections from the Carmina Burana   A verse translation by David Parlett

The famous songs from the *Carmina Burana* (made into an oratorio by Carl Orff) tell of lecherous monks and corrupt clerics, drinkers and gamblers, and the fleeting pleasures of youth.

Fear and Trembling   Søren Kierkegaard

A profound meditation on the nature of faith and submission to God's will which examines with startling originality the story of Abraham and Isaac.

Selected Prose   Charles Lamb

Lamb's famous essays (under the strange pseudonym of Elia) on anything and everything have long been celebrated for their apparently innocent charm; this major new edition allows readers to discover the darker and more interesting aspects of Lamb.

The Picture of Dorian Gray   Oscar Wilde

Wilde's superb and macabre novella, one of his supreme works, is reprinted here with a masterly Introduction and valuable Notes by Peter Ackroyd.

A Treatise of Human Nature   David Hume

A universally acknowledged masterpiece by 'the greatest of all British Philosophers' – A. J. Ayer

FOR THE BEST IN PAPERBACKS, LOOK FOR THE

PENGUIN CLASSICS

A Passage to India   E. M. Forster

Centred on the unresolved mystery in the Marabar Caves, Forster's great work provides the definitive evocation of the British Raj.

The Republic   Plato

The best-known of Plato's dialogues, *The Republic* is also one of the supreme masterpieces of Western philosophy whose influence cannot be overestimated.

The Life of Johnson   James Boswell

Perhaps the finest 'life' ever written, Boswell's *Johnson* captures for all time one of the most colourful and talented figures in English literary history.

Remembrance of Things Past (3 volumes)   Marcel Proust

This revised version by Terence Kilmartin of C. K. Scott Moncrieff's original translation has been universally acclaimed – available for the first time in paperback.

Metamorphoses   Ovid

A golden treasury of myths and legends which has proved a major influence on Western literature.

A Nietzsche Reader   Friedrich Nietzsche

A superb selection from all the major works of one of the greatest thinkers and writers in world literature, translated into clear, modern English.

PENGUIN CLASSICS

Honoré de Balzac	**Cousin Bette**
	Eugénie Grandet
	Lost Illusions
	Old Goriot
	Ursule Mirouet
Benjamin Constant	**Adolphe**
Corneille	**The Cid/Cinna/The Theatrical Illusion**
Alphonse Daudet	**Letters from My Windmill**
René Descartes	**Discourse on Method and Other Writings**
Denis Diderot	**Jacques the Fatalist**
Gustave Flaubert	**Madame Bovary**
	Sentimental Education
	Three Tales
Jean de la Fontaine	**Selected Fables**
Jean Froissart	**The Chronicles**
Théophile Gautier	**Mademoiselle de Maupin**
Edmond and Jules de Goncourt	**Germinie Lacerteux**
J.-K. Huysmans	**Against Nature**
Guy de Maupassant	**Selected Short Stories**
Molière	**The Misanthrope/The Sicilian/Tartuffe/A Doctor in Spite of Himself/The Imaginary Invalid**
Michel de Montaigne	**Essays**
Marguerite de Navarre	**The Heptameron**
Marie de France	**Lais**
Blaise Pascal	**Pensées**
Rabelais	**The Histories of Gargantua and Pantagruel**
Racine	**Iphigenia/Phaedra/Athaliah**
Arthur Rimbaud	**Collected Poems**
Jean-Jacques Rousseau	**The Confessions**
	Reveries of a Solitary Walker
Madame de Sevigné	**Selected Letters**
Voltaire	**Candide**
	Philosophical Dictionary
Émile Zola	**La Bête Humaine**
	Nana
	Thérèse Raquin